"Get down!" he yelled, reaching over to push Holly's head down toward the floor for cover. "Someone's shooting at us!"

There was the *plink* again as another round struck the glass near where his head had been only moments before.

He grabbed his radio to reach out to 911 as he flipped on his concealed red and blue lights and the siren. "Shots fired. Shots fired. Near the corner of 34th and Main. Send all available deputies."

There was the crackle of the radio and the 911 dispatcher's response. Units were on the way.

He reached behind his seat and pulled out his rifle, then slapped the magazine to make sure it was seated. "Don't move. Stay low and behind cover. I don't want you getting hurt. You understand me?" He stared at Holly, who looked wide-eyed with terror.

"Who is shooting at us?"

He shrugged, but he had a feeling he knew exactly who was pulling the trigger—and who was about to go down in a blaze of gunfire.

ACKNOWLEDGMENTS

This book and all those in this series wouldn't have been possible without my strong support team at Harlequin. They constantly strive to keep me growing as an author while making each book better than the last.

Also, thank you to the members of the Missoula Search and Rescue Team for taking the time to show me around the facility and responding to my many questions while writing this series. I couldn't have done it without you.

WINTER WARNING

DANICA WINTERS

Harlequin
INTRIGUE

Thank you to all who put their lives on the line to help others.

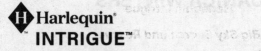 **Harlequin®**
INTRIGUE™

ISBN-13: 978-1-335-45682-3

Winter Warning

Copyright © 2024 by Danica Winters

For questions and comments about the quality of this book, please contact us at CustomerService@Harlequin.com.

TM and ® are trademarks of Harlequin Enterprises ULC.

 Harlequin Enterprises ULC
22 Adelaide St. West, 41st Floor
Toronto, Ontario M5H 4E3, Canada
www.Harlequin.com

Printed in Lithuania

MIX
Paper | Supporting responsible forestry
FSC® C021394

Danica Winters is a multiple-award-winning, bestselling author who writes books that grip readers with their ability to drive emotion through suspense and occasionally a touch of magic. When she's not working, she can be found in the wilds of Montana, testing her patience while she tries to hone her skills at various crafts—quilting, pottery and painting are not her areas of expertise. She believes the cup is neither half-full nor half-empty, but it better be filled with wine. Visit her website at danicawinters.net.

CAST OF CHARACTERS

Detective Ty Terrell—A sexy, hard-nosed detective who can't stop acting against his better judgment after he and his Search and Rescue team find a beautiful skier who is a blast from his past.

Holly Dean—The incredibly professional and competent owner of Spanish Peaks Physical Therapy. She is as wild as she is stubborn, but no one can say she doesn't live life to the fullest. Unfortunately, her cavalier attitude sometimes gets her into some sticky situations.

George "Moose" Dolack—An adventurous deputy at the Madison County Sheriff's Office and a member of the Big Sky Search and Rescue team who has a mama who loves him more than life itself.

Valerie Keller—A member of the Big Sky Search and Rescue team who loves to help but has a horrible habit of never telling anyone no—especially when it comes to her sister.

Evelyn Keller—Valerie's sister and a woman with a checkered past and an unpredictable future.

Robert Finch—A womanizer who has Holly squarely in his sights, even though she has repeatedly told him she isn't interested.

Chapter One

The skier had been missing since last night. In these sub-zero temps, death had likely found the skier long before Search and Rescue had even been notified.

Ty Terrell could count on his fingers the number of times they had managed to pull people off the mountains alive after that amount of time. If he had to guess, the skier had gone off path and found themselves in a slide. Avalanches happened with striking regularity in the Spanish Peaks outside Big Sky, Montana.

If this missing skier had gotten wrapped up in a chute, then they wouldn't be found until the snowmelt next spring—if then.

He blinked and an image of the last body he'd found in the thaw popped into his mind. The guy had been discovered still frozen, looking like a Peruvian mummy with his lips curled tight above his teeth, his eyes sunken and his skin browned by the ravaging effects of prolonged cold. He'd looked nothing like the pictures of the fifty-three-year-old man they had been sent to find. Aside from being freeze-dried, the guy had been in pristine condition. His wallet had even been in his back pocket, which had made identification that much easier.

Hopefully this SAR mission would be different, and it

wouldn't be a recovery, but a rescue—even if the feeling in his gut told him it was likely the former.

He checked to see that his black Trunab go bag was in the back seat of his pickup as he started the rig. It was a long drive up to the trailhead, one made longer by slick roads, which may or may not have been plowed this week. It had snowed last night, which would make this rescue even harder, but hopefully they could still pick up a track at the location where the skier had put in and then simply follow the ski marks.

The drive up to the Beargrass Trailhead normally only took about ninety minutes from his place, but today it took closer to two hours, even driving faster than he should have. Thankfully, until the last half mile or so, he had been able to keep it out of four-wheel drive even though the snow was more than two feet deep in some spots. Someone else had cut tracks through the fresh powder and as long as he stuck to them, he'd been good to go.

At the trailhead, Cindy DesChamps, Chad Tenley and George Dolack—who everyone lovingly called "Moose"— were already sitting there waiting for him with the sleds as he pulled up. They looked annoyed, or maybe it was that they were amped to get working and each passing second was another heartbeat closer to their victim expiring.

He pulled his truck up in front of their rigs, making sure not to block the trailers so they could get in and out as they needed. Moose walked up to his window. "I didn't know I needed to call my mother to drive your ass up here." He slapped his hand on the edge of the open window. "Could you have gotten here any slower?"

"Hey, man, you're lucky I made it here at all. I just got off work," he said, picking up his Search and Rescue beanie and slipping it over his slightly too long brunette hair. He needed to get it cut—if he ever had any down time.

"Did you get all the texts about our vic?" he asked.

In all honesty, he'd just heard they were looking for a woman who'd gone missing while skiing. That's all he'd needed to hear. "Of course." He waved Moose off.

Moose rolled his eyes but didn't bother to ask questions. He knew Ty well enough by now that he didn't have to worry. Ty always completed his mission. "A few members are already out there, working the bottom line."

"I swear, I got here as quickly as I could."

"Just because you're some fancy-pants detective, you think it's some kind of excuse for being half-informed and late," he huffed, with a teasing laugh. "I see how it is."

"You know I would much rather spend time talking to you and Cindy than chasing down felons and doing high-risk stops."

"Yeah right, *high-risk stops*," Moose repeated with a laugh. "The only high-risk stuff you've done in the last six months is testing your stomach at the little taco truck near the ski hill."

"Those tacos are *amazing.*" He rolled up his window. The guy wasn't entirely wrong. He'd been spending far too much time in his squad car serving warrants and answering repeat offenders' assault calls. It was all pretty routine, although he would still have to say that everything he did came with inherent risk. Though, it wasn't anything close to what most people saw on cop shows on television.

Big Sky was made up of mostly ski bums in the winter, hunters in the fall and fish heads in the spring and summer. Crime always came with people, but his little town didn't have an abundance of either. He had to admit that he liked life just as it was.

He stepped out of his warm pickup and the cold stung his face. It was going to be a long day on the mountain. Going to the back of his rig, he grabbed his snow gear and donned up. There was no such thing as cold, there was only having the wrong clothing to deal with conditions. That being said, he hoped he'd brought the right coat and pants. According to the radar, it was supposed to dip into the double-digit negatives tonight and tomorrow, which would only be compounded by the wind speed on their sleds—it would easily feel at least fifty below in a matter of minutes. Hopefully they'd find this skier before having to worry about the nighttime temps.

The team had the machines unloaded and he clicked on the comms, which fed directly into his helmet. Cindy was on her sled and, after testing to make sure they could all hear each other, they hit the trail.

He turned on his heated gloves, trying to keep up with Cindy who was riding fast and hard on the ridgeline. According to the map, the ridgeline ran flat then gradually descended into the valley below. If a person was proficient, they could work the line basically back into town, though it would take about a day.

Maybe the skier was just going slower than anticipated. Or, she had gotten started later than she had intended.

They moved to the side of the tracks as the trees grew thicker. If the skier had been in this thick stuff the entire way, he and the team would have to work around the main area where she had disappeared, making large circular swaths where they could look for exit points instead of sticking exclusively to the trail. It would make their search far harder, but they would do what needed to be done.

If all else failed, they would have to come in on their skis, but it would make any sort of recovery more difficult. If things went that direction, he wouldn't be surprised if they had to call in the helo team to airlift out their victim.

"I'm going to take the middle trail," Moose said, motioning to the right with his hand. "I'll meet you guys at our first waypoint."

"You got it," Cindy said. "We will expect you there in one hour. Let us know if you need assistance."

"Roger." Moose tipped his hand in acknowledgment before running his sled toward the bottom of the far tree line.

The run he was taking was far more treacherous than Ty was comfortable with, but he could understand Moose's thinking. It was a perfect chute for a skier who wanted or needed to make a faster descent. Even though there was solid logic behind his decision, he didn't like that Moose was going alone, but Cindy was the boss. Besides, Moose was the most experienced rider of the group, and if anyone was going to make that run, he was their best choice.

Thanks to the sound of his own engine, he could barely hear the roar of Moose's sled as he rode off into the distance, but everything would be fine. Expanding their search perimeter was the best thing they could do, regardless of his personal feelings. They could get to Moose pretty quickly if they needed to; Ty just needed to stop being overly cautious.

He took a breath of the exhaust-scented air and pushed forward behind Cindy and Chad. These two had been dating for a while now, and they weren't about to leave each other's sides. He loved that level of commitment. He'd kill to have that kind of relationship, someday. He'd have to meet the woman of his dreams first, and to this day the only woman who'd ever come close was his very first girlfriend, Holly Dean.

They'd been fifteen when they started dating and they'd been together for most of high school—until she had decided to run off to college and leave him behind. He'd tried to fight the fight and tell her that he'd follow her, but she hadn't wanted him. That had been that.

Everyone had told him that time would heal that wound, but all it did was serve as a reminder that losing love was the worst kind of pain.

He found the thoughts reawakening parts of him that were best left dormant, and he pushed the memories down.

After thirty minutes, the tracks reappeared near the base of the copse of trees. Cindy radioed, "Looks like we're back on trail."

"Roger," Moose answered, "meet you below."

He had definitely been overly cautious. Maybe he'd seen too many injuries and his line of work was taking a toll on him. Though crime wasn't too bad around Big Sky, just last week he'd been first on scene for a man who had been smoking while installing a propane tank in his grill. It hadn't ended well for his nose or his fingers. Hopefully the guy didn't need all ten digits for his job.

Maybe Ty simply needed a vacation—somewhere tropical.

As he dreamed of palm trees the snow drifts grew around him, and to his left there was a large subalpine fir with a tree well so deep he didn't dare to approach.

If he had to guess snow here had to be at least ten feet deep in some spots. They were over the bottom limbs of the trees now. It was wild.

The tree growing by the large fir shook violently. He slowed down, braking. That was odd. As he looked closer, the base of the small tree was covered in something red. It wasn't just red…no, it was ruddy and pink. *Blood.*

He stopped his sled. "Cindy, we have movement back here," he radioed.

He didn't want to move too close to the fir, and if there was someone stuck at the base of the shaking tree, he didn't want to cause a cave-in. They'd have to be dang careful as to not cause further issues than those they already faced.

He turned off his engine and pulled off his helmet. As soon as he did, he heard a muffled woman's cry.

"Ma'am, I'm on my way. I hear you!" he called, not so loud as to cause problems with avalanches, but loudly enough that he hoped she would know help was on the way.

He put his helmet down and climbed off. After grabbing his pack and his shovel, he did one last check that everything was there and easily reachable if there was a cave-in or other emergency. Her muffled cry grew louder.

Cindy and Chad turned to come back to him as he slowly moved toward the woman's call.

He started to dig about six feet back from where the woman's cry sounded. Cindy radioed Moose and the lower team to let them know they'd located their vic. Moose didn't answer—they'd have to update him when they met at the waypoint.

After making the calls, Cindy and Chad parked back by his sled and grabbed their shovels. As they all set off to work, it didn't take long for them to be waist deep in the snow pit. Cindy talked nonstop, reassuring the woman that they were coming and everything would be alright.

It was amazing how just simple communication could help ease a victim's terror.

The woman's voice grew louder as he neared her. He put his shovel to the side and started to scoop back the snow with his gloved hands. Two purple-gloved fingers poked through the snow to him. He took hold of her fingers and pushed back the snow. The woman's helmet came into view. Even though her face was mostly covered, he recognized those blue eyes—Holly.

Before the shock of seeing her could settle in, he had to stay focused on the job at hand. "I've got you." He'd always had her. Even when he didn't.

She nodded, but her eyes grew wide as she recognized him, as well. "Thank you, Ty."

"Don't worry, we are going to get you out of here and to the hospital for care," Ty said, trying to bring her comfort in this time when she needed it the most.

He reached down under her arms and pulled her back from the tree and into the pit his team had created. She fell back into his lap as he landed in the snow.

"How are you feeling? Are you hurt?" he asked, panicked.

She shook her head. "I'm fine. A little cold, but I'm okay."

"Were you skiing alone?" Chad asked.

Holly was shaking, but he wasn't sure if it was from hypothermia setting in or from the adrenaline of being found. She tried to remove her helmet, but her hands were barely functioning, so he helped her pull it from her head.

"It…being alone…it was a mistake." Tears welled in her eyes. "I knew better."

When she sat back, blood poured from her thigh. They had to get her to the trucks and warmed up and her wound looked at as quickly as possible—though they had found her, her life still hung in the balance.

Chapter Two

Holly had never been any good at following directions, especially when people told her to be quiet, to step back and let others take the lead, or to stay in her lane. To listen was to have her soul silenced, which was far worse than being reprimanded for having a voice. However, this was a lesson in humility.

She should have listened.

However, the conditions were perfect for the day on the slopes. Fresh powder and sunshine. What more did a person need?

Her co-owner at Spanish Peaks Physical Therapy, Stephanie Skinner, had told her that the slopes were looking treacherous, but *no*…she had to be headstrong.

Well, that had definitely come back to bite her right in the butt.

Now she was waiting on a Search and Rescue team to return in the passenger seat of her ex-boyfriend's truck—the same ex who had just come to her rescue—while holding a compress to the outside of her thigh. Plus, she had broken her ski. Altogether, this was going to cost her *big*.

Her thoughts moved to the movie *Pretty Woman* and the moment Julia Roberts said the word.

A giggle escaped her lips. The sound pulled Ty's attention and he glanced over at her, making her realize how ill-timed her laugh had likely sounded. He'd once called her emotionally unstable when they had been together. Her wayward laugh likely only reminded him of how unstable she really was…validating his past accusation.

Gah… I have already given him enough ammunition to use against me, she thought. *Then again, he can think what he wants to think.*

No matter how good-looking he was, or how, when she looked over at his pink lips, she could still recall the way he kissed—slow and hungry and so full of passion that the mere thought made her squirm—yeah, no matter what, his opinion of her didn't matter.

"You getting warmed up?" he asked, adjusting the heat vents so a steady flow of hot air poured out on her.

She was burning in more ways than one. He didn't need to know that, though.

She nodded and cupped her fingers over the other immediate heat source and let it pour into her palms until it burned, and her fingers felt as though they were being stung by bees.

"Thank you, again," she said, not quite sure what to say to the man from her past who had risked his life to save hers.

"I'm glad we got to you in time. We had been told you were missing since last night," he said. "I didn't even know your name. Your coworker had just reported that you had failed to show up for work and he had been told you'd been skiing."

That sounded about right, Robert Finch would make an emergency call like that without talking to others. But in this case, his overprotective nature had been to her benefit. When it came to her, he was less than rational. Lately, though, his attentions had been moving toward their administrative assistant—who he cared about *a little too much*.

"I meant to go out yesterday after work, but I waited until this morning instead. I'd told my co-owner, Dr. Skinner, I wouldn't be in the office today, but Robert mustn't have heard." She pressed her warm hands against her chilled neck, and it made goose bumps rise on her skin. In what seemed like seconds, her hands were cold again and she pressed them back over the heater.

She hated being cold, but she couldn't complain after how close she had come to turning into an ice cube.

"Wait." She paused, looking over at Ty. "So you didn't know it was me you were looking for?"

Ty shook his head. His dark hair was longer than the last time she had seen him, and it fell into his chocolate-colored eyes. She had always thought he had the most beautiful hair of any man she'd ever seen—it was unfair, really. Why did dudes always have the best hair when all they had in their showers was a steadily shrinking bar of green soap?

"No, like I said, I didn't." He gave her a look that wasn't exactly soft but made it clear that he didn't mean to come off as a jerk, either. It was like his coming out there to rescue her was just *business*.

She didn't know if she should ask him the question that was nagging at her, but she couldn't help herself. "Would you have come if you *had* known it was me out there?" She motioned toward the hillside where he had dug her free of the snow.

He cringed slightly like he was trying to dodge a wayward bullet.

She was nothing if not direct. It had been one of the

reasons why they hadn't worked. He was far more pas-
sive while she dealt with things as they popped up—who
knew such a thing could be a fatal flaw?

He sighed, like he was thinking about the same thing
and was reminded of why they would never work out—
even though many years had passed since the last time
they had spoken. "My job requires that I do what is
needed of me. And, if you remember correctly, I wasn't
the one who broke things off between us. I don't have
any hard feelings."

He was lying. There was no way he hadn't resented
her for her saying what they had both been thinking at
the time—things between them just weren't what they
needed to be in order for them to move forward as a couple. At the bottom of it, in high school, they both still had
some growing up to do.

Now, well…maybe he'd changed. Maybe he really
didn't have any hard feelings and she was the one who
was still living in the past.

"Let me take a peek at your leg," he said, changing the
subject and pulling her out of her world of whodunit and
whys. Some hatchets were best left buried.

She pulled back the gauze, exposing a long slash on
the inside of her thigh where her ski had snapped and
cut through her snow pants. Now that the bleeding had
slowed, she could tell that it would have been well-served
with a couple of stitches, but regardless of whether she
chose to get them or not, the wound would heal. She
hated stitches.

"It's going to be all right—I can tough it out."

He leaned over and pushed back the edges of her
black snow pants so he could get a better look at the
semi-staunched cut. "We will have the doctor look at

it—though it looks like you didn't hit the femoral artery. When we first got you out, I was a little worried. It looked like you lost quite a bit of blood."

"You know it often looks way worse than it is." She replaced the gauze and pulled her pants back over her cut, covering her skin.

"It looked like you would have died without me." He sent her a strained grin.

She wanted to deny the truth and tell him that she would have been fine, but when she closed her eyes and paused for a moment, she was struck by the terror of being under the weight of the snow. She could still feel the pressure of it on her chest.

Her breathing quickened at the mere thought.

Being suffocated by snow had always been one of her greatest fears. She thought about the heaviness of the snow on her chest and the inability to struggle free of the concrete-like icy snow every time she had been out skiing, but thankfully it had never stopped her.

She wondered how she would feel the next time she skied, or if there would even be a next time.

"Are you okay?" he asked.

Dammit if he didn't always have a way of knowing exactly what she was feeling right at the moment she was feeling it. It was like he could pick up on her emotions even better than she could sometimes.

"Yeah." She sounded airy, even to herself.

"You went through a lot today. I'm sorry if I made you feel badly about it." He messed with the heater vent again, more out of some need to expend nervous energy than it was to help either of them, she assumed. "I...I was just surprised to see you. And, for your information, I would have kicked myself if I had not come out here and then found out it was you who needed help after the fact."

She forced a smile. He was only playing nice. "You don't have to say that, but I appreciate the sentiment."

He frowned and there was an uncomfortable silence between them that made her realize what a misstep she had made and how she had sounded.

He opened his mouth to speak, but she raised her hand to silence him. "I didn't mean that… I'm sorry."

His eyes widened.

"I really am grateful it was you out there. I am humiliated that I even found myself in that situation. I'm a better skier, I know not to get close to the trees, but…" She ran her hand over her face.

"Nature and life have a way of humbling us all." The corner of his mouth quirked up in a tired, c'est la vie grin. "You did see your skis, right?" he said, motioning to the broken ski in the back of his truck.

The sight brought a tear to her eye as she nodded.

She could understand humility, but she hated being constantly humbled in front of this man.

His handset crackled and there was a garble of sound as a woman spoke. Strangely, he seemed to understand, but to her it was nothing more than women's tones and static.

"I'll be waiting," he said, letting go of the button on his handset as he stared at her. His eyes were wide and for a brief second, he looked…well, *lost*.

"What happened?" she asked, fear creeping up within her.

"Moose, the other member of my team, hasn't checked in. He was going to meet us at the end of the draw at Beargrass. Cindy and Chad have been sitting there waiting for him, but he's still not arrived." There was a crack in his voice.

"When was he supposed to be there?" she asked.

He glanced at his watch. "Almost an hour ago."

She didn't want to ask if he thought something had happened to his teammate; it seemed ridiculous. Of course, something had gone wrong if the man wasn't showing up on time. These people were professionals, and they were known for their promptness and higher level of communication if, and often when, something went awry.

"Hand me some duct tape." She motioned toward her pants.

"You can't go out there with me. You're cold, hurt, not trained, and I don't have room on my sled." He sounded adamant.

He could keep her plenty warm.

"Look, you guys were out here for *me*. Make room on your sled." She opened up his glovebox and inside was a roll of tape. "Ha! Some things really never change."

"It's simply planning ahead," he said, sounding almost annoyed.

She took a piece of the tape, ripped it free and closed the gap in her pants. "Let's go. Your friend needs help. I'll be fine."

Even as the words left her lips, she felt the falseness in them. She wouldn't be fine, not as long as she was forced to be so close to the man from her past. Every second with him was a second her heart was in danger.

Chapter Three

Ty had to be out of his mind. There was no way he should have let her get on his sled with him, but there they were… him driving the sled with her sitting behind him with her arms around his waist. He could think of a hundred reasons why this was a bad idea, but the single reason to say yes—that his best friend was missing—was enough to make him act against his better judgment.

Besides, Holly was the most stubborn woman he'd ever met. If he tried to argue against it, he'd spend the next hour talking and she'd still probably get her way. It was better to just bite the bullet and put Moose's needs ahead of his own.

He glanced back at Holly, who was tucked down behind him to lessen the wind on her face. It was smart, but somehow her blond hair flipping around annoyed him.

Then again, most things about her annoyed him. Spending time with Holly was akin to nails on a chalkboard. Everything she did drove him up the wall. She was hardheaded, brusque and always thought she was the only one who had the right answer. With her, it was her way or the highway.

Truth be told, though, when her mask fell away, she was also one of the most caring and giving people he had ever met. And even now, after all these years, he couldn't deny the fact that she was stunningly beautiful. A piece of her hair caught the wind, and he watched it flip around as he drove. He could still remember how soft it had felt the nights he had run his fingers through her locks.

"You doing okay?" he asked, slowing down and tapping her on her uninjured leg to get her attention. She was wearing his helmet and it was a little big, but he hadn't allowed her on without at least some level of safety gear that covered her entire head. They had already saved her once; he didn't need to put her life in danger any more than necessary once again.

She nodded, the helmet loose and wobbling on her shoulders so much that she stilled it with her hand.

It was cold without his helmet, but as long as she was good, so was he. He pulled his beanie down farther over his ears.

He sped up, trying to follow the tracks in the snow in front of them in his bouncing headlights. Riding at night was always fun, but it came with an entirely different set of dangers—sticks became lances and cracks in the snow were like steel traps. Added to that danger was having her on his back, which affected the sled's balance and stability in the deep snow.

He tried to control his nerves. From the get-go on this call, things had just been *off*. Maybe he was the one who had caused this all to go a little sideways.

It will be fine. Moose is going to be okay. He tried to talk himself down off the ledge.

He and Moose had been friends since they had gone to the law enforcement academy together. Moose hadn't risen up the ranks like he had; he had jumped around from department to department because his wife at the time hadn't loved living on the east side of the state. She needed mountains, or so Moose said. They'd ended up here, but as soon as Moose had gotten a house, the wife had served him divorce papers.

Now he'd been working in Big Sky for about a year and the divorce had finally been settled.

For the last six months, Moose had been going through what Ty could only call Moose's groupie phase. He'd taken more women home in the last few months than Ty had in his entire life. That was, until recently when, according to Moose, he'd found a good one.

How good? Well, this was Moose he was talking about so that was up for debate.

He slowed as they started down the steep grade at the end of the ridgeline, near the location where they had found Holly.

Holly.

She squeezed him as they passed by the area where he and his team had found her. He wondered how it made her feel. If it had been him, he would have been embarrassed, relieved and grateful. He kind of got those vibes from her, but there was something else there that he couldn't quite put his finger on.

Her arms loosened around him and, as they did, he found he had almost liked them tighter. He was tempted to turn and tell her to hold on more, but he restrained himself. Things between them were already weird enough without him making things worse.

As they drove, and he cut back and forth on the mountain, he couldn't believe he found himself this close to her once again. She was one girlfriend who hadn't left his thoughts, but he had never imagined running into her. She was out of his league, and always had been.

The last time he heard anything about her, she had been dating an anesthesiologist out of Bozeman. The guy had been jet-setting around the globe with her, and he'd seen a few pictures on her social media of them standing on the different islands around the Pacific Rim between ski trips in Vale and Whistler.

If she was dating those kinds of guys, he wasn't sure why she had even come back to make her home in Big Sky. On a positive note, she was working as a physical therapist at a local place. Maybe she liked to keep a certain level of her own autonomy and independence without being beholden to some jackass anesthesiologist.

Whatever it was, and whether or not she was still with the dude, it was none of his business. He needed to simply keep his mind on watching the overhanging branches and downed logs—though, he had a feeling that those weren't the only dangers he faced.

Cindy and Chad were parked at the first location, and as he pulled up, he found them munching away on protein bars and energy gels like they knew, just as well as he did, that it was going to be a long night.

"Hey," Cindy said, watching Holly as she took off his helmet and slipped it under her arm. "I'm glad to see you were up for a ride. You must be feeling better. How's the cut on your leg?"

"It's just a flesh wound. Nothing major." Holly smiled, reassuringly. "Thank you for everything. Seriously, I'm sorry for what happened."

Cindy waved her off. "It's what we do."

Chad, Cindy's boyfriend, nodded. "Besides, we love coming up here. It's fun…until something like this happens. Though—" he paused, looking over at the trail leading from their location "—I'm sure we will find Moose.

Knowing him, he ran out of gas or something. He *was* in charge of his own sled today. You know how he can be."

Ty chuckled, but the knot in his gut didn't go away.

"The other team we had working the bottom are heading home," Cindy said.

"How many were there?" he asked, trying to play it cool. That was what he got for being late this morning and not asking more questions.

"There are four on the other team. Frank Vallenti, Valerie Keller, Dan Wood and Smash—don't ask how he got the nickname, you know it involves women." Cindy put up her fingers like she was counting.

He liked the other members of SAR, but he hadn't worked with Valerie or Dan much. Smash was hilarious and, on a few occasions, they had put some down at Stockman's Bar. He didn't drink much anymore, but if Smash invited him, he was going to be there. The guy had a way of speaking that reminded him of a Southern grandpappy, especially when he had a ZYN nicotine pouch under his lip.

"They haven't heard from Moose, either," Cindy continued. "We were waiting for you guys to catch up, then we are planning on everyone working the face of the mountain. We will meet at the bottom in two hours. If you find Moose, radio in. Cool?"

"Make sure you stay in contact. We don't want anyone else going missing," Chad added.

Ty nodded, watching as Holly slipped on his helmet and pushed her blond curls under the edges. She really was beautiful.

He grabbed his extra set of goggles from under the seat and put them on his head. His cheeks were still exposed, and they would get cold, but it was better than nothing and at least Holly was going to stay warm.

They hit the slopes again, working around the side of the mountain and into the timber. He drove slower than he normally would, taking his time especially around the trees as he made sure not to get anywhere near their bases. If he turned off the engine and came to a stop, he was sure that he would have been able to feel Holly's heart thrashing in her chest. After all she had been through, she was taking this getting-back-on-the-horse thing like a real trouper.

The snow started to fall, and the wind picked up, making it appear like they were in a shaken snow globe thanks to his headlights. It was so dark and the world around them felt muffled, even dampening the roaring sound of their engine.

Holly tapped his shoulder and he pulled to a stop. He turned. His face was achingly cold, and his lips were starting to chap. He looked back at her. "Everything okay?" he asked, wondering if something had come over the comms or if she was hurting or something.

She pulled up the helmet so he could hear her. "Do you have a flashlight?" she asked.

He reached into his chest pocket. "I have a headlamp," he said, pulling it out. "Why? Did you see something?"

"I just need a minute," she said, reminding him that she was human.

He handed her the light, clicking it on. "I'll step over here," he said, motioning to the right. "Don't go too far. The snow is soft in places. I don't want to have to dig you out, again."

She didn't laugh. Instead, she gave him a little nod as she affixed the lamp and stepped off the sled.

Walking out into the storm, he thought about how he had been wrong in teasing her. It was too much, too soon. If she remembered anything about him at all, it was that joking around was how he tended to deal with anything uncomfortable. It was what made his job as both a SAR member and a detective bearable. If anything, he wished he could be funnier—like Moose.

When they found him, Moose was going to be the butt of the jokes around the unit for a while. The last time Moose had done something foolish was when he'd taken a header off the team's raft and had lost his radio and a myriad of other electronic gear at the bottom of the river. They had called him the million-dollar baby for months, even after their divers had managed to retrieve some of the lost gear.

He figured he'd take advantage of the moment while Holly was doing the same and climbed off the sled. He moved to unzip his pants, but as he did, something caught his eye. There, near the base of the fir, was the tip of a ski. It was yellow and at a strange angle, and he recognized it as the bottom of one of the SAR unit's sleds.

"Moose?" he asked, calling out into the blizzard.

There was no answer.

The knot in his stomach moved up into his throat and, as he tried to call his friend's name again, it came out as a croak. He moved nearer to the exposed ski on the machine. He pulled out his cell phone and turned on the light, exposing the world around him. About ten feet past the downed sled, lying under a slowly melting patch of snow, was a body-shaped lump.

Moose's blue jacket was sticking out and a few feet from his right hand was his helmet.

He moved toward his friend, instinctively knowing what he was about to find.

Even in his wildest imagination, he couldn't have been prepared for this…

Moose's head was nearly cut off. His eyes and mouth were opened wide as though he had been frightened to death and he was forever left screaming.

Ty was forced to look away.

He looked toward Moose's feet. Even under the fresh snow, he could see the pink tinge of blood; it was nearly everywhere he shone his flashlight. Moose hadn't been dead long—just over an hour at most.

If only he had gotten here sooner. However, even if he had, in the case of an injury like this, there would have been nothing he could have done for his friend.

He took a series of photos with his phone, making sure to get the entire area around the body. He even took a shaking video. In an environment like this, where there was fresh snow coming down and windy conditions, it wouldn't take long for the entire scene to be covered and any evidence destroyed.

He continued rolling the video as he moved to his best friend's body and brushed off the thin layer of snow from his jacket. His jacket was cold and the heat from his body had dissipated. The coat was covered in blood and nearly black. In the bright light of his flashlight, it was hard to see, but it didn't really look like he'd sustained any other injuries. However, until they got the coroner in, it would be hard to say with absolute certainty and he wasn't about to disturb the scene any more than required.

After confirming his friend was deceased, he took a step back and said a silent word in honor of him. It helped the pain in his chest, but nothing could make that heartache go away.

The snow beneath Moose had soaked up the blood and melted from the warmth of the liquid, but it appeared to have gotten chilled enough that everything sat still—and the only sound was of the falling snow and the wind.

Thanks to the melting of the snow, Moose's head was tilted back at a strange angle, exposing the sliced flesh. He could make out the rubbery edge of the severed windpipe. Thick red clots of blood had pooled at the edges of the cut and had slithered down his trachea like deathly red snakes.

The angle of the cut was nearly perfectly straight, no slashing or sawing. It was almost as if Moose had run into a wire…or, someone had wanted him unquestionably dead.

Chapter Four

Holly tried to control her breathing, but as she took in a long inhale, the taste of blood filled her mouth with its coppery tang and she slammed her lips shut. *This*…this man's death… It was her fault.

She'd left the privacy of the trees only to stumble upon this scene. Now she glanced down at the nearly decapitated body, then quickly turned away.

Yes, there was no denying he was dead.

Her stomach roiled, threatening her with a wave of nausea, but she tried to swallow it back.

Why couldn't she have just gone to work? Instead, she had been selfish and decided to take the day off and play. Look what it had cost the world around her…

"Ty…" she said, barely whispering his name.

He looked over at her, but there was a vacancy in his expression that made her wonder if he was really even hearing her or if he was acting on instinct alone.

"Ty, I'm so, so sorry." She didn't know what to say, or how to say it. She was rattled by her role in his friend's death. "I wish…I wish I could bring him back." *And take back this entire day.*

This was all something out of her worst nightmare. She'd always feared getting hurt on the slopes, but even in her terror, she had never imagined that it would be followed up with something like this—an innocent man losing his life.

Ty grunted, looking away.

He was so reserved, but even in his stoicism, she could feel his pain radiating from him. Or maybe it was anger.

She clamped her mouth shut. Anything she could say to him now, well…she was worried that it would only make things worse.

His handset crackled to life as Cindy said something over the comms. Ty frowned and as she caught his eye, he turned away, shielding himself from her gaze. It bothered her more than she cared to admit.

"We located Moose. DOA." There was a metered stoniness to his voice.

Cindy said something on the other end of the mic, and though Holly couldn't make out the words she was saying she could hear the sadness in her tone.

This wasn't just Holly's worst nightmare—it was all of theirs.

TY WAS TRYING to hold back all the rage that filled him. He wanted to yell at the sky and tell the world what a screwed-up place it was. How could this have happened?

He had to get his act together. Anything he was feeling would have to wait.

Ty exhaled, long and hard, collecting himself. He was a detective first and a friend of Moose's second.

He couldn't fall for the torrents of anger that raced through him. For Moose's sake, and for the sake of his family, Ty needed to handle this situation with as much professionalism as possible.

That meant, for right now, until he knew more about

what had actually happened, he needed to treat this area and the body like it was a potential crime scene. Which meant he needed to notify the sheriff and let him know what had happened. Hopefully, Sheriff Sean Sanderson would make the call to Moose's mom, Rebecca. However, if anyone should notify her of Moose's death, it should be him. He was his closest friend and he'd eaten dinner on many a Sunday at Rebecca's home. They were close, so close in fact that she sometimes called Ty her adopted son.

He found himself getting choked up thinking about the woman who, just like him, was now alone in this world.

Knock it off, he reminded himself, closing off the door to his emotions once again.

There were some things and some aspects of this that would have to wait.

One step at a time.

He turned to Holly. "Are you okay?" He should have asked her before, but like a jerk he'd been so caught up in the hierarchy of needs that she'd had to wait.

She nodded, but he could tell by the darkness in her eyes and the slump in her shoulders that she was lying to him. While he appreciated her attempt to shield him, he was the one who should have been shielding her.

"Why don't you walk over here with me, if you'd like?" he asked, holding out his hand.

She turned to his gloved hand with a slight look of surprise, but then slipped her hand into his.

Their footfalls crunched in the hard, frozen crust of the snow beneath them. The wind was kicking up, causing the temps to plummet. He led her just far enough away that she couldn't see the body but to a point that was still visible from a headlamp's light beam.

"First, none of this is your fault." He took her other hand and made her face him.

She wouldn't meet his gaze.

"Look at me, Holly," he ordered.

She shook her head and from the trembling of her hands, he could tell that she was struggling to keep her emotions under control—he knew that feeling all too well.

Something about her struggle made him steel his resolve. Holly needed him to be the strong one. For her, he would.

She looked into his eyes, her gaze filled with guilt and pain. "You are okay." He tried to calm her.

"I'm… This… It's my fault." Her voice was strangled. "I should have just gone to work."

He took hold of her hands, and the action was so unexpectedly comfortable that it caught him off guard and he struggled to keep his train of thought. "Moose is… *was*…a good friend of mine." He motioned his head in the direction of the man's dead body. "I can promise you that he wouldn't want you to take responsibility for this."

"Someone will. I'm sure his family and his *wife* will want answers." She choked on the word *wife*.

He couldn't help the little chuckle that escaped him at the thought of Moose still married. Moose would have had all kinds of colorful words at that kind of talk.

However, the thoughts of Rebecca once again gave Ty pause. "His mom is one of the kindest and most generous women I know."

"That doesn't make me feel any better…" She paused and looked down at their entwined hands. "Not that I should."

"That's not where I was going." He wanted to pull her

chin up, to make her see his face and know he was telling her the truth, but things between them were already more intimate than he intended. There were some things he just couldn't deal with today, and not having a clear head with this woman was one of them. "Look, seriously, we don't even know what has taken place here. We need more answers before you can start condemning yourself."

His handset crackled to life and Cindy's voice pulled him from Holly. He'd have been lying if he said he wasn't a bit relieved. It was hard to console her and tell her not to feel guilty for her role in this, when he was feeling the same kind of culpability within himself. He was the one who had let Moose go out on that trail alone. He'd even questioned it at the time. If only he had spoken up or agreed to ride with him. Sure, the trail he'd taken was more challenging, but if Ty just hadn't been a wimp Moose might still be alive.

Cindy was two minutes out. He was relieved, but he wished he could stop anyone else from feeling the same way that he and Holly were. As soon as they showed up, he held no doubts that they would be as troubled by Moose's death. Moose had been a friend to pretty much everyone in their unit. This was going to hit the team *hard*.

He needed to talk to the sheriff.

"Holly," he said, squeezing her hand, trying to comfort her as best he could. "I need to make a phone call. I don't want you going near the remains, okay?"

She nodded, but she said nothing. Her silence did little to help the stone in his gut.

"I'll be right back. Cindy is on her way."

She nodded again but let go of his hand and moved to sit down on the top of the snow at his feet. In all reality, she probably needed the rest. She'd had one helluva day. He could only imagine all the things that she was thinking and feeling—and compounding it all had to be hunger and sheer exhaustion. He should have never brought her back on the mountain. However, choices had been made, and things had turned to this. There was no going back, there was only moving forward. And maybe that was what he should have said to her about her guilt. Hell, it's what he needed to tell himself, but he wasn't about to take his own advice to heart.

He pulled out his cell phone. Surprisingly, given their location in the backcountry, he had service. He tapped the contact for Sheriff Sanderson. Without a doubt the man was going to hate hearing from him this late at night— a call at this hour only brought bad news, and a whole helluva lot of work.

"What's happening?" Sanderson answered the call on the second ring, not bothering with the niceties that most outside of the law enforcement community abided by and considered polite.

"There's been an incident." He tried to sound placid and cool, not giving anything more than what was required.

There was the rustle of what sounded like bedding in the background of Sanderson's call. "What kind of *incident*?"

He swallowed back the lump that had moved into his throat and threatened to choke back his words. "Well, we found the missing skier, but Moose didn't make the waypoint. We went back in and looked for him… I'm sorry to tell you, sir, but Moose is dead."

There was a long pause. "What happened? Do you know, yet?"

"Not yet. We located his body and got a positive ID. His head was almost perfectly severed…too neatly to have been an accident. I was hoping that you could call in an agency assist." He treaded carefully, not wanting to step on Sanderson's toes by telling him in even the slightest way how to do his job.

"On it. Send me your exact coordinates. I'll have a coroner there as soon as possible. Where is the rest of your unit?"

"We sent everyone home who wasn't needed. I figured they could get some rest." Ty sent his commander their location.

"Good." The sheriff sounded tired.

"You should have our pin."

There was a click and the sound on the other end of the line changed as if Sanderson had put him on speakerphone so he could operate his phone and talk clearly at the same time. There was a buzz. "Yep, got it." There were a few thumps, like Sanderson was tapping on his phone. "Coroner has been dispatched to your location. I'm going to call our partners at DCI to see if they would be willing to handle the investigation. I'll be in touch."

"Yep."

"Terrell," Sanderson said.

"Yes, sir."

"Don't you dare move. And I don't want a word of this leaking out, at least not yet."

The man hadn't needed to tell him. He was in his position for a reason, but he appreciated that his superior wanted to keep this under wraps.

Chapter Five

As Holly sat on the ground and stared out at the snow, there were soft murmurs behind her as Cindy and Ty spoke. They were probably talking about how she shouldn't have been here, and what a burden she had become.

No… I need to stop feeling sorry for myself, she chastised. *I caused this man's death. I just need to take responsibility and make amends.*

How could she make amends, though. There was no bringing this man back or telling his family that time would heal all wounds. She knew all too well that such an old adage was nothing more than an attempt to mollify those who needed to feel more than anyone else. Besides, time did nothing more than add distance from the sharp pain of immediacy. It did nothing for the memories or the soul-crushing moments when the losses unexpectedly took over in full force.

She knew that feeling of all-encompassing loss too well. She'd lost both of her parents in a car accident on I-90 just five years ago. The thought of their deaths still haunted her. And in moments like this, where she was facing death, it brought all the memories of losing them rushing back.

She stared vacantly at the snow-encapsulated world

around her as she thought about how much she missed her mother's gregarious laugh—a laugh she would never have the chance to hear again. And her father, he used to love to drop dad jokes like they were going out of style. She loved to hate them when she was a teenager, but now she would have given anything to hear him make a crack.

The snow glistened in the moonlight, sparkling like her mother's eyes when she had laughed at her father, and it made her heart ache.

The trees were covered in a layer of snow that made them appear exactly as their namesakes—snow ghosts. She stared vacantly at two stripes in the snow. They led off into the distance over the hill and disappeared into the darkness of the night. There was a snow sled track in the center of the ski marks, reminiscent of a tank track.

She followed the marks toward Moose's body, expecting to find his machine at the end. However, instead there was a spot where the machine had been parked and someone had gotten off. The footprints in the snow headed toward the body, and in the snow was a well-packed area and then Moose's sled ski.

The marks were *strange*. It almost looked as though two sleds had been in the area. Yet, she didn't recall Ty saying Moose had been working with someone else.

The wind kicked up the cold, powdery snow, making it spin like someone had shaken a snow globe with her sitting at its center.

The only people who knew they were in the area were the people who had been looking for her. Did that mean that someone from this guy's team had murdered him? Or, at the very least, played a role in his death?

The thought tormented her.

Her negligence had brought this man up here, which made her complicit in this man's death.

She was never going to forgive herself.

She tried to shake off the feelings, though. Self-flagellation was only going to take this thing so far and none of it would be in the right direction.

Besides, there was no way one of his teammates would want him dead. So far as she knew, the Search and Rescue team was just a volunteer group. If someone hated someone else, then why would they stay and keep volunteering? And all of these people had to be the type who were selfless—they were donating their time, bodies and equipment to rescuing people like her for nothing more than a "thank you" and a "good job" at the end of the day. They hardly fit the profile of killers.

This had to be nothing more than a horrible accident. Nothing else made sense.

Ty walked over toward her, his footfalls crunching in the snow as he approached, and he cleared his throat like he was afraid of interrupting her thoughts. "Holly?" he asked.

She turned to face him. "Hmm?"

"You ready to head back to town?"

She frowned. Not long ago, he'd made it clear that he hadn't wanted to leave the scene, but now he was ready to ship her out.

"If you want. We can go." Though part of her wanted to stay and help, she wasn't sure what she could do, and she was getting more tired by the minute.

"Actually, I'm going to send you out of here with Cindy. I can't leave the scene unattended." His face was barely visible in the thin moonlight, but she could see the tiredness in his eyes and hear it in his tone.

"I can wait. There's no need to make Cindy pack me out. I'm fine."

"I know you are okay, but I need to make sure you're fed and that you stay safe. I'm sure you're aware, but it gets cold out here at night. I bet your adrenaline from the day has worn off." He knelt down next to her. "I can see you shivering."

Until he'd said that, she'd not really thought anything of it. In fact, she'd barely noticed. She must have been going through an adrenaline dump. Though she had seen others go through them after especially painful or intense physical therapy sessions in her clinic, she'd never gone through something like it herself. She held a newfound appreciation for her patients—heck, maybe she'd go a little lighter on them the next time they came in for their appointment.

She looked over at Cindy, but as she did, Cindy looked her way and blinded her with her headlamp.

"If we go…you'll be here alone." She tried to control the quaking that was starting to intensify throughout her body.

He looked back in the direction of Moose's remains. "I appreciate your concern, I really do. But this is what I do, Holly." There was a tenderness to his voice that she hadn't heard come from him in many, many years and it tore at her.

He was hurting and there wasn't a thing she could do about it—even if he'd wanted her to stay by his side. It only served as a reminder of how out of each other's lives they had become and would likely continue to be.

She nodded. "I get it."

There was an unexpected tightness in her chest, almost as if by leaving him on this hillside she was once again excising herself from his life.

Her feelings didn't make sense—even to her. They had broken up. They weren't *anything*. Yet here she was yearning to be by his side. What was she doing?

She glanced one more time out at the tracks as he helped her to standing. Her gloved hand fit perfectly in his and it only made the confusing feelings within her intensify.

"Did you see those?" she asked, nudging her chin in the direction of the tracks.

He looked over and his head moved to the side, reminding her of a cute puppy. The likeness of which didn't help her mixed feelings about him.

"That's strange…" He looked at the tracks that led over toward Moose's machine. He pulled out his phone and started to take pictures of the scene like she had watched him do with the body.

"I'm surprised you didn't notice them," she said, not really thinking about what she was saying. "I mean you're a detective. I thought you'd have noticed them right away."

The cuteness in his demeanor shifted and a darkness that had nothing to do with the night filled his eyes. Instead of saying anything, he turned away.

Her stomach clenched. That had come out all wrong. That's not what she'd wanted to say… It was just that she never thought he'd miss such a thing given his profession. She cringed at her thought. Of course, she'd meant what she'd said, but why did she have to be so tactless sometimes? Why couldn't she have simply been helpful and left it at that. Instead she had to run a sliver under his fingernail.

She watched him walk away, but she didn't call after

him—there was nothing for her to say that could fix what she'd just fractured between them. It was really no wonder that he had broken up with her those many years ago. She'd never really had a way with words, but apparently time hadn't changed that as much as she had hoped.

A few minutes later, Cindy came walking over and handed her what she knew, thanks to the red markings and "Terrell" stenciled on the back, to be Ty's riding helmet. She thought about not taking it, or maybe refusing to ride back, but she accepted it and followed Cindy as she directed her to her sled and motioned for her to get on.

As Cindy started the engine, Holly looked back at Ty who was watching them. He gave her a stiff nod and she slipped on his helmet, fully aware that this was their last goodbye.

Chapter Six

He watched as they placed Moose's remains into the coroner's van. This would be the last time he saw his friend, and the realization broke him like he would have never thought possible. With Moose gone…he was on his own. Moose had been his greatest friend. They had spent so many years hunting, fishing and drinking beer together that without him, Ty wasn't sure he wanted to do any of their favorite things ever again.

To do it without Moose, it just didn't seem right.

The doors slammed shut, pulling him from what he now realized were inane thoughts. Here he was staring at the body bag and thinking about standing on the banks of the Madison with the man whose body was growing ever colder.

Those memories and choices could wait, even if the thoughts wanted to press through and take him to the best moments he'd once had with his friend.

He dropped his head and closed his eyes as the van took off down the icy road, careening slightly as the back tires worked to find grip. The van spewed black smoke like it was some kind of pissed-off bull.

Anger filled him as he listened to the van's tires slip and the engine rev—if they weren't in such a hurry, they would have been able to navigate the ice without issue. While there wasn't anything else that could happen to Moose that could make him more dead, it struck him as wrong that the coroner was so irreverent. On the mountain, he and his team had treated Moose with absolute veneration and care and to see the coroner fishtailing and spinning his tires tore at him.

He turned toward his truck and trailer, his sled already loaded, and he was ready to go. It had been a long day.

Getting in his pickup, he pulled onto the slick road, careful to ease on the gas and not repeat the moves that the coroner's van had made. The thought of the coroner's driving made him shake his head again.

Then, how could he judge the guy when he hadn't been perfect on this call, either. He had basically dismissed Holly—and that was after he had agreed to let her come along to find Moose. Had he known things would have gone so sideways, there was no way he would have brought her along. However, the last thing he had ever expected was to find Moose like that…with his head nearly completely severed. Who had done this? And why?

As he envisioned the blood-soaked snow, he pressed the gas pedal a little too hard and he was forced to slow down. He tried to think about anything other than all that blood. It had been everywhere…everywhere except near his sled.

That fact could mean any number of things, but one likelihood rose above all the rest—Moose hadn't been sliced on his sled. His death had to have come after he'd stepped off.

He had searched around in the dark, but he hadn't seen anything obvious on scene that fit an object capable of what he had found. Hell, he hadn't even found a stick.

The last time he had been called out to a death reminiscent of Moose's was when he had been a deputy. A man had run into a wire while riding his mountain bike and the results had been nearly identical. Which made him think that there had to have been something out there that he simply hadn't seen.

There had just been so much blood.

He ran his hands over his face and picked up his phone as it buzzed with a series of emails and messages from the unit and the sheriff's office. Everyone was texting him and sending their condolences. He wanted to tell them that they were sending them to the wrong person—they needed to be talking to Moose's mom.

Then again, he needed to talk to her first—he'd have to be on her step at dawn so no one would make a mistake and have to bear the weight of tearing down a mother's world.

He looked at the sleeves of his jacket. Though he'd been wearing nitrile gloves while working on the scene, he'd still somehow managed to get his friend's blood all over his arms.

It was hardly the first time he'd had blood on him from a crime scene; he was constantly covered by the detritus of crime and death, and the sight of it didn't bother him. If anything, it felt…well, *not right*, but somehow cathartic. If anyone in the world should have been out there on the mountain taking care of Moose in his final physical form, then it was him.

He wasn't into the woo-woo stuff, but he couldn't help but wonder why Holly had come back into his life at the same time. It had to be some kind of message from the universe or whatever.

It was strange that on all the calls in all the years he had been doing this kind of thing, he'd never worked with an ex, and he'd never before lost a best friend. It had to be more than a coincidence, though he couldn't make sense of what else it all meant.

Not long after they'd broken up he'd been lost, and it was then when he decided to apply to work at the sheriff's department. He had met Moose at the academy in Helena.

Damn. Holly had even been behind his meeting his best friend in the first place.

It was wild how many things in his life were connected to her and their failed relationship.

Maybe it was only right that she had been there when Moose had passed—though, she could have never known all the threads that connected them. In fact, she probably hadn't even known Moose. She hadn't said anything to make him think she had, but she had been through so much that anything was possible.

Hopefully she was going to be okay—emotionally and physically. She was pretty tough. Heck, if he had to guess she had never gone to the hospital or gotten stitches.

The thought made him almost smile and huff a laugh, though he couldn't have told anyone why. Maybe it was the fact that she was exactly what every Montana woman was bred to be—tough as nails and capable of handling everything from a blown-out head gasket to a rattlesnake in the garage. Then again, they were also the kinds of women who, when they got all gussied up, could wear Chanel and walk the streets of New York City with enough confidence that people assumed they were locals.

He had to admit he had a thing for that type—the *Holly* type.

He had only spent a handful of nights with Holly. Yet he found that when he was lonely, it was those nights which he found himself thinking about. She had been a one-of-a-kind woman when they had dated, and she had become more of everything since they had parted. She was definitely the one who got away.

It did him no good to sit here and rehash the old days, when he had so many other things that he could be dealing with. One thing was for sure, he needed to find out what exactly had happened to his friend. As far as he was concerned, that was where all of his attention needed to be focused.

However, it wouldn't hurt to swing by Holly's place and check on her on his way home. That way, he could find out whether or not she had arrived safely and if she had in fact gone to the hospital. He owed her that much. Heck, he didn't even need to stop—hopefully, she'd be sleeping by now and a porch light would be on or something. If he did stop by, would it be weird? It kind of felt weird.

He tried to reassure himself by repeating the fact that he simply wanted to make sure she was safe. He would have done it for anyone. It just happened to be that this *anyone* was Holly.

It seemed like she was an exception to a lot of his rules—or maybe it wasn't rules, but comfort zones.

Once he had heard that comfort zones were where the human spirit went to die. Maybe she was being sent to him or placed back in his life to be some cosmic reminder that he needed to grow as a person. He just wasn't sure which direction.

As he drove the miles back into town, his mind did double backs and somersaults as he thought about how he should approach things with Holly, or *if* he should approach things. He was making a huge assumption that she would even want to have him back in her life. She hadn't

seemed like she did. Yet she had touched him. That had
to have meant something.

As he entered town, he thought about getting her number on their database and texting her, but he didn't even
know what to say.

Hey, how are you doing? No.

Doing okay? No, too clipped.

Worried about you. Too much.

His best bet was just to swing by.

He exhaled, hard. He resigned himself to the fact that
there was no right move here, there was only doing what
his heart was telling him to do. He turned left down Spring
Road, and toward the house where Holly had grown up
and of which she'd eventually taken ownership when her
parents had passed away—or so he'd heard through the
small-town gossip mill.

It had started to snow harder, and he clicked his lights
down to low beam so he could see through the flurries
in the dark slightly better. His eyes were tired and as he
eased down the road, the snow crunched under his tires.

He couldn't ignore the nagging in his gut that was
telling him to turn around and that he had no business
checking up on her. However, it was too late to turn back
now. If he did, he'd spend all night worrying about her
and second-guessing himself. It was only going to take a
second and then he could get some damned sleep.

Tomorrow was going to be just as arduous as today
had been—tomorrow, the investigation would go into
full effect.

As he neared her house, he spotted a white King Ranch
heavy-duty pickup parked across the street. It didn't look
like anyone was inside.

The 1970s-style house hadn't changed much on the

outside since he was a kid. The only difference had been new gray siding, which did little to mask the age of the place. It wasn't his business, but he wondered if Holly had updated the inside when she had taken over ownership of the house, or if she had left it as her parents had kept it—with the brown and white textured carpet. The carpet where they had lain on their bellies, casually touching feet while they had pretended to watch television. He kind of hoped she hadn't changed a thing.

Her SUV was in the driveway, making him wonder how she had gotten it home—the last he'd seen, it had been parked where she had gone in on the ski trail. Cindy must have made sure she'd gotten home with it, or she'd had someone drive it back for Holly.

As he drove closer, her front door came into view and standing in front of it was a man with dark hair. He was wearing a heavy winter coat and cowboy boots. Ty didn't recognize the guy, but he slowed down as he watched the man bang his fist against the door. Every time he banged his fist against the wood, the Christmas wreath hanging at its center shook violently and the glass bulbs looked dangerously close to flinging off and crashing to the ground.

The guy pissed him off. Perhaps it was his intensity to get Holly to answer the door. There was a doorbell, but the guy seemed adamant about beating up the structure.

Ty slowed his truck to a crawl.

Before he reached the King Ranch pickup, he pulled to the side of the road, just far enough to be unobtrusive and unnoticed, but still see the front door and be accessible if something was happening and she needed help.

The man wailed on the door again, this time kicking at the bottom when his knocking went unanswered.

Ty reached for his door handle, readying to go have a talking-to with the unknown man as Holly's front door opened. She appeared in the light, a dark frown on her face. She was wearing a white nightgown that hugged at her frame like wanting hands, and it made her appear almost angelic in the snowy night.

She crossed her arms over her chest, but whether it was from the cold or fear, Ty wasn't sure.

Whatever was going on here, he didn't like it.

He kept his hand on the handle of his pickup, but he didn't open his door. Before he went rushing out to save her, he needed to make sure that she was really in need of saving and that he wasn't rushing in where he wasn't needed and acting like a fool.

The dark-haired man leaned against the doorjamb, moving in closer toward Holly. She stepped back from the man, but she didn't close the door. If the man was as bothersome as Ty was assuming, he would have thought that Holly would have slammed the door in the man's face. Instead she stood there talking and as she spoke her hands lowered from her chest. She looked more re-laxed, but suddenly the man she was speaking to stood up straight and waved his hands in the air—the move was aggressive.

She put her hand on the open door like she was about to close it, but the man stuffed his foot inside the door as he continued to wave his hands wildly. Ty rolled down his window, hoping to hear something to tell him whether or not his presence was justified here, or if he was just witnessing a lover's spat.

The only problem was, she hadn't mentioned that she'd had a boyfriend, or even hinted that she was in any kind of situationship or whatever. Sure, it had not been his business, but from the way they had touched, and she hadn't pulled away, he assumed that he was cleared for landing…well, not *landing* her, but at least for seeing if she wanted to go out and have coffee sometime.

The man's yelling cut through the air. "Don't you care about anyone besides yourself?"

She put her hands up and her face pulled into an even deeper scowl. "All I've said is that you can't just show up here."

The sound of the man's hand connecting with the doorjamb was Ty's call to arms. That was it. He jumped out of the pickup and raced over toward Holly.

As she spotted him, her face brightened for a split second before she took on a look of utter confusion. The man with his back to him turned. "What in the hell are you doing?" the man asked, but then as quickly as he spoke, he turned back to Holly. "Is this your new boyfriend? I should have known. You always had a thing for dumbasses."

"Are you sure you didn't catch a glimpse of yourself in the glass, buddy?" he said, nudging his chin toward the door but never taking his eyes off the man.

"Funny," the guy said, turning around to face him. He looked like he was about thirty-six, and he was pale but carried the kind of bulk that made it clear he worked out. He could still take him.

"Knock it off," Holly said, moving outside, her face coming fully into the porch light. "You need to leave. You've been drinking," she said to the guy. "And you—" she turned to face him "—what gave you the right to think you could show up on my doorstep in the middle of the night and be my knight in shining armor? Haven't you done that enough today? I think you need to leave, too."

He was taken aback. She wasn't wrong, but she sure as hell wasn't right—he was not a knight and he hadn't come here to save her. "Holly, I just wanted to make sure you were okay. I needed to know you made it home. That's all."

"I'm here. You can go, too."

"Holly—" He said her name like it was a call to her for forgiveness and a whisper of something more. It made him feel weak in front of the other guy.

The dude put his hand on his shoulder and Ty instinctively jerked away from the guy's touch. The man smirked. "You know…if you want her more than me, you can have her. She is manipulative and cruel. Pushing me away and pulling me back—"

"How dare you," Holly started.

The guy put his hand up, quieting her. "Before I go, though, let me say one more thing," he said, sounding drunker than ever, "this soul crusher is nothing but problems. I'm doing you a favor in telling you to tuck tail and head out, man."

"I've always been a man who makes up my own mind. More often than not, when someone says something like you just did, it means one of two things—you're jealous or you are angry that you'll never have a chance. In this instance, I think it must be a combination of both."

The guy moved abruptly like he was about to strike, but before he did Holly made a squeaking noise that stopped the guy in his tracks.

"Robert Finch and Ty Terrell." She said their names in a way that reminded him entirely too much of his mother. "You both need to get off my porch!" She stepped between them. "Neither of you get to pick and choose what I do with *my life*."

He stood there in stunned silence.

She looked up at Robert and then to Ty, anger flaming in her eyes. "I said *leave.*"

Chapter Seven

Rebecca Dolack answered the door in her oversize floral nightgown even though it was nearly 9:00 a.m. Ty was glad that he hadn't decided to come over in the middle of the night and wake her up to tell her the news of her son's passing. She deserved one last good night of sleep. For the foreseeable future, she would be dealing with all the things that came with death.

"Ty, good morning!" she said, touching her silver hair, which was mussed from sleep. "You should have told me you were coming, kiddo—I'm all a mess." She smiled at him for a moment, but then she must have picked up on his concern and hesitation. Her smile disappeared. "What happened?"

She glanced over his shoulder at his pickup like she was looking for Moose. He hated that she would never see him walking toward either of them ever again.

"Mrs. Dolack, I'm so sorry to have to inform you that Moose passed away last night." His voice cracked and he couldn't help the tears that started to slip down his face.

She dropped to her knees as a wail escaped her, the sound like that of an injured animal—instinctive and so lingering that he knew it would forever haunt his dreams.

He sat down beside her, pulling her into his arms as

she sobbed. He said nothing. There were no words that would make the pain she was feeling any better. Nothing could stop the agony that came from having a soul torn apart.

HOLLY HADN'T MEANT to come off like she had, but the entire situation had taken her by surprise. She had no idea why Robert showed up at her house claiming that he had been so worried about her, and he felt he needed to rush to her aid. He was constantly telling her how he didn't need her, that she was garbage and in the way. Then the next minute, he was telling her how much he loved her and needed her.

He was all over the map, but then he'd accuse her of the same thing. Yet, the only thing she had ever done was tell him no and that she wasn't interested in any kind of relationship. They worked together—and for all intents and purposes, she was his boss, though the way the company was structured it didn't feel that way. Even if they hadn't worked together, he wasn't her type.

He was always making it a point of telling her that he had more women than he knew what to do with. From what she was led to assume, there was no amount of Viagra that could keep him satisfying them all.

Thankfully, they'd seemed to finally come to an understanding a month or so ago that he wasn't interested in her or she in him. Unfortunately, the second she started getting interest from other men he'd shown back up in her DMs. He was such a creep.

No doubt his appearance on her doorstep had more to do with the liquor he'd been drinking than his actual feelings. He didn't care about her; he'd told her as much. He did, however, seem to care about the administrative assistant at their physical therapy office. Maybe she had been the one behind his calling about her being missing.

Regardless of his motivations, Robert had no business at her house. They weren't a thing and they would never be a thing. They worked together, they were civil, and that was all it needed to be.

What she really couldn't make heads or tails of was Ty.

She hadn't even known he had come down from the mountain. From the way he'd made it sound, he had intended on being on the scene for a while. Additionally, from the way things had ended between them, even if he had been back in town, she hadn't expected to see him ever again. Let alone him showing up on her doorstep. If she hadn't been so embarrassed by the situation she was dealing with, she perhaps would have taken the time to ask him why he was there.

Though he had said he was there to make sure she'd arrived home safely, she couldn't come to terms with why he thought rolling up on her and her coworker was appropriate. The only thing she could clearly see was that he had a savior complex.

She hated to admit it especially given what had happened, but it was sexy that he wanted to come to her aid even though they weren't, and would never be, in a relationship again. He was just a good guy, even if his actions weren't quite in line with her expectations or assumptions. And maybe that meant the problem lay somewhere with her.

She tried to think about the situation from his perspective. Robert had been angry. He'd been intimidating and punchy, but she knew well enough that Robert was only being demonstrative, and he'd never do her any harm. He was just bigger than life sometimes.

At least, she didn't think he'd really want to hurt her.

From Ty's point of view, she could almost understand why he thought he needed to swoop in and save her. Unfortunately, he'd caught her off guard and she had responded poorly. At the very least, she owed him an apology.

That night had been fitful, but she had tried to find some sleep before she had to go to work the next day. Her thoughts kept moving between Robert and Ty and how she needed to deal with both of them, but she was left with more questions than answers.

She probably needed to call the Search and Rescue unit and thank them for coming to her aid. However, she wasn't entirely sure that she was ready to speak to Ty or anyone associated with him. Not only was she embarrassed about last night and Robert, but she was also embarrassed for having ever needed their rescue in the first place. Added to that was Moose's death and everything else, and it was clear she had created an unimaginable situation.

She felt so guilty.

Nothing she was doing was right. She never wanted to be that girl. She was thirty years old and creating more problems than ever before in her life. Her grandfather used to say that "when you found yourself in a hole, sometimes the best thing to do was stop digging." This time, not only did she need to stop digging, but she needed someone to take away the excavator she seemed to be doing it with.

The clinic was busy this morning and so far, Robert hadn't shown up for work. According to Penny Reynolds, the assistant, she had yet to hear from him. Penny had said nothing about what had transpired between him and

Holly last night, so she had to assume that Penny knew nothing about it.

She wasn't about to expose their ridiculous melodrama and cause more issues.

Besides, if Penny had been going out with him then she had to have known what kind of guy he was. He never made it a secret that he was a womanizer, even going so far as to hit on women in front of her and Penny. So far, he hadn't done it to a patient, as that would have been Holly's line in the sand. She had made that known to him, as well. What he did in his private life was his business and had been up until the point he had tried to include her. Last night definitely changed some dynamics, and they would need to face things head-on.

It was really no wonder he wasn't in a rush to get to work this morning.

After seeing her third patient of the day, an eighty-seven-year-old man with severe sciatica, Penny called her from the front desk. "There's a delivery up here for you," Penny said.

"I'll be there in a second," she said, resenting the fact that she would once again have to be close to Penny today after everything that had happened. It wasn't in her nature to walk on eggshells.

Robert was going to pay for this.

Maybe she could find a way to get Dr. Skinner to agree with her to fire him, or something. She couldn't stand being around him and her ability to withstand him was waning by the day.

On the other hand, if he hadn't acted yesterday, she wouldn't have been alive today. In a way, she owed him her life.

She made her way to the front of the clinic. There were

two other, newer physical therapists working today. One was in the pool near the back, and she could hear the murmur of his voice and the splashing of water as he worked with his patient. The small therapy pool gave the place a chlorine smell, but she liked it. The aroma made her feel like they were doing more than most in their field and that they weren't afraid to do what it took to make sure their patients had the highest levels of care.

She really was proud of her business...that was, as long as she didn't delve too deeply into the personal lives of the other owners and staff.

She sighed as she neared the front desk.

Personal lives were personal; she just had to leave everything there.

"Hi, Penny," she said, forcing a smile. "You have something for me?"

Penny smiled widely, her perfect white teeth sparkling in the lights, and she nearly bounced in her chair. Though they weren't that many years apart, she seemed so much younger. "Look." Penny pointed at a large bouquet of red roses and white lilies.

The scent of the lilies wafted over her. She loved lilies. "Did you see who brought them?" she asked, her thoughts moving to Robert. He was probably sending her flowers to the office to apologize for his behavior and to soften her for when he showed up at work—eventually.

"The Peaks Floral shop just delivered them," Penny said. "But there's a card, right there. Hurry. Open it. I'm *dying* to see who they are from." She clenched her hands together and held them to her chest like a kid waiting to open their Christmas presents.

Holly was half surprised that Penny didn't just stand up and hop from foot to foot in her excitement.

It was silly, but she didn't want to open the card in front of the woman who was clearly more excited about the flowers than she was. She appreciated them, but in every bouquet or unexpected gift, there was always some kind of hidden cost. If these were from Robert, the price would be forgiveness—and she wasn't entirely sure she was ready to pay.

Maybe she was just jaded.

She'd have to watch out for that in herself. Jadedness led to bitterness. To her, there was nothing worse than a bitter person; they were toxic as their resentments and anger had a way of spreading to those around them like slow-moving cancer.

"Aren't you excited?" Penny asked, obviously noticing Holly's demeanor.

"Who wouldn't be excited for flowers?" she answered, pasting a smile on her face and trying to be nice. She walked over and sniffed the lilies, taking pleasure in them for a moment before solving the mystery of the sender and then having to unravel their intended meaning.

She plucked the white envelope from the card stand and slipped the card out. All it said was, "I'm sorry." There was no signature, and it looked as though it was in a woman's handwriting—which she had to assume was the florist who had taken the order.

She sighed.

"Oh…" Penny said. "Is it a juicy note? You going to let me read it?"

She was surprised Penny hadn't already. If she had, she was faking it well.

"Someone is apologizing." She forced a smile and turned away, leaving the beautiful flowers on Penny's desk. The last thing she wanted to do was spend the rest of the day in torment whenever she spotted them. Whoever had sent them was going to be in more trouble for not signing the card than if they had sent nothing.

If they were from Robert, she'd once again need to tell him that he held no place in her private life. If they were from Ty...well, she'd need to tell him the same thing— and then follow it up with her own apology.

Chapter Eight

The office was buzzing when Ty rolled in. Everyone was standing around in the bullpen talking about what had happened on the mountain. Valerie, a member of SAR and who worked as an evidence tech for the department, was sitting next to their new hire, Heather Lazore, a twentysomething woman, in the corner trying—but failing—to conceal her sobbing. Her face was buried in her hands and her shoulders were rounded and bobbing as she cried. Valerie was patting her back and trying to console her, but her face was expressionless.

Ty considered going over to console the woman and take over for Valerie, but he struggled to understand this reaction. She hadn't worked there long enough to have been in Moose's bed.

Her reaction was over-the-top and he had to walk away in order to not dislike her for her outburst. When he hurt, he only wanted to be left the hell alone.

Moose wouldn't have wanted a public display like hers, a yowling false lamentation. If the tables had been turned, and he had been the one to die, Moose would have probably already been cracking jokes about his final fiery destination.

He smiled at the thought.

A lump formed in his throat as he thought about Moose. His emotions threatened to get the better of him, but he suppressed the urge to feel. Action was always the answer.

In the academy, he'd spent weeks learning that inaction only meant one thing—death. He didn't want to test that lesson.

One of the other detectives, Detective Leo West, waved at him and motioned to Ty's office. The day of closed-door meetings was about to happen. He internally moaned. He needed to be out on the hill, hitting the investigation in full force, not sitting in his office and handholding.

He nodded at West, putting his finger up and letting him know it would be a minute. First things first, he needed to be the leader the sheriff had wanted him to be. "Hey, guys," he said, loudly enough to get everyone's attention. He hadn't prepared to do this, but someone had to say something about what had happened and his shoulders were wide enough to bear the weight.

"As all of you have heard by now, our brother in blue George 'Moose' Dolack has died." He stopped, thinking about how much he hated the word *died*. It didn't feel right. Moose hadn't merely died, he left everyone under circumstances that none of them wished upon even their greatest enemies. "The sheriff has let me know that there is a counselor available for anyone to go to and talk about what has happened. I strongly urge you to take this opportunity to seek help and get things right within you. We are all equal members of this department and, as such, we are only as strong as our weakest member. Be strong, take care of yourself and take care of your team. If anyone needs to talk to me—" he motioned at West again "—I will be in my office and available whenever my door is open."

Heather's cry pierced the air, but she choked it back,

making it sound strangled and high-pitched. She lifted her hand and excused herself from the work area with Valerie by her side.

He felt for her, he really did, but he was glad to see her go. Hopefully, she would be the first one to see the counselor about her feelings.

As he walked toward his office, he looked in the window. There was a blonde sitting in the hard blue plastic chair right across from his desk. He didn't recognize the back of the woman's head, but seeing anyone in his office and waiting for him when he first arrived made his stomach clench.

This day just kept getting better.

He turned to West who was tagging along behind him. "Looks like someone already beat you to the punch." He nudged his chin in the direction of the woman in his office.

"I need to talk to you about this Moose thing." West looked serious, but then when it came to this incident, most were. His gaze moved in the direction of the wailing Heather and Valerie.

"I'll be with you as soon as I handle *this*." He sighed.

West looked hesitant, as though whatever he wanted to talk about was of the utmost importance and he couldn't give up easily.

"I promise," Ty added, trying to reassure the guy.

Finally, West seemed appeased.

He cleared his throat before he stepped into the doorway of his office. The blonde turned to face him, and she had a surprised expression on her face as though she hadn't been expecting him even though she had been sitting in his office.

Holly.

He was shocked to see her. Of all the people he would have guessed to find sitting in his private sanctum, the last person he would have predicted was the woman who had recently kicked him out of hers.

"Ty," she said, making his name sound even more clipped than it was.

"How can I help you?" he asked, walking in and closing the door behind him. His heart was racing as though he was walking into an interrogation, but the one being interrogated was him.

"I think I should—"

"Apologize?" he said, cutting her off. "Don't worry about it. As far as I can tell, you and I were always on different pages. Since we have known each other, we have never quite fit into each other's lives when and where we think we should."

She quirked an eyebrow and stared at him like she was searching his face for answers. "You think you should fit into my life? Now?"

He ran his hand over his face and stepped behind his desk, leaving his back toward her for a second longer than necessary in order to gain control over his mouth. He turned. She had a tiny smirk on her lips. "That's… I just mean you and I—"

"Just stop," she said with a smile. "I know what you mean, I only wanted to watch you try to explain yourself. I've thought about *us* since you helped me up there, too. It's normal to dredge up the past when put into situations like we were. That doesn't mean anything needs to come from our thoughts. We are old enough to know we are incompatible—at best."

He sighed, the simple action was like a pressure valve on his soul. If she thought they were *incompatible* then he didn't need to delve into any of his feelings. Things between them were not going anywhere and he could focus on everything else going on in his life. "You were always one to be direct."

"I find it can help to face some things head-on." She squirmed, like she was thinking about something, and her gaze moved to his desk.

He'd put everything sensitive out of sight and locked away, but he suddenly felt overly exposed for a variety of reasons. "By the way—" he paused, shuffling loose interoffice memos someone had placed on his desk "—who let you into my office?"

"Don't worry," she said, her smile disappearing. "I haven't been here very long and the other guys in the office never really left me alone. I don't think they wanted me touching anything. Oh, and I didn't if that's what you are worried about."

He had been concerned about that, and whoever had let her in without his being inside was going to get an ass chewing. No one needed to be in his office when he wasn't present. At least he knew she could be trusted. She wasn't the one at fault, and she certainly didn't need to feel guilty about someone else's misstep.

"That's not what I was thinking at all," he lied. "I was only wondering."

She sighed, but he didn't think it sounded like it had come with a sense of relief. "The woman at the front desk brought me back, Heather was her name I think."

"Got it." He scowled but caught it and tried to cover it up as he thought about all the things he was going to say to their new hire. "So, what brought you here today? Is there something you need my help with?"

She looked almost affronted. "I…I wanted to apologize, whether or not you wanted to hear it. And I wanted to explain about what happened last night—"

"You made it clear...we are *incompatible*. If that's the case, you don't really need to explain what happened. You and your *friend* were having an argument. I shouldn't have been there. I shouldn't have interceded. I was wrong, even if my intentions were good. It's fine. I learned my lesson," he said, shutting her down.

One thing was certain, he wasn't about to apologize. He may have made a mistake in acting on his instincts, but he would do it again if he was ever in a similar situation. The key was not to let himself get in a position where he had anything emotionally at stake, again. And that... that was easy enough if he only kept his distance from the woman who'd planted herself in his office.

"I appreciate that you acted. I do." She wrung her hands, nervously. "The guy you saw, he's not my boyfriend and he's not really interested in me, he just had way too much to drink."

"I could definitely tell he'd had too much to drink. However, the rest of what you said I don't believe. Even if you're not currently in a relationship with that guy, he seemed to think that you should be." He tried not to sound annoyed, but he couldn't stop it from entering his voice. "Regardless, it doesn't matter who he is to you. And I don't think that you need to worry about coming here and explaining your situation with him to me. Let's put it in the past. I'm sure he was worried about you, that was obvious."

"Robert has made it clear that he would like to have more than a working relationship, but I'm not interested."

Oh, this just kept getting better.

"Was he the guy who called you in as a missing person?"

She nodded her head. "I'm surprised he did. He has women all over him and I really thought he was over this little crush on me."

"Would you say that that kind of behavior was normal for this guy?"

She shook her head. "He really isn't a bad man. He just doesn't always think things through."

"Oh, I have to say, if this was me, I wouldn't be working with someone like that."

"Well, it's a small town, and I haven't been an owner long enough to hire and fire at my leisure."

"Are you trying to tell me that as smart as you are, you don't have options?"

She crossed her hands over her chest, the universal sign that she was done talking about this. He couldn't blame her—this was uncomfortable. Whatever she chose to do in her love life was up to her. It was none of his business. "Look, I didn't come here to be judged by you or to seek life advice."

"Then why *did* you come here? You've apologized, so…" He glanced toward the door.

He was being a jerk, but she had hurt his feelings and he couldn't help himself. He could only put up with so much, and she was testing his limits.

"I want to help with this thing with your friend."

"No." He started to move toward the door to make it clear that it was time for her to go.

"Hear me out," she said, raising her hands in a desperate plea.

He paused, though he should have kept on moving.

"I know I'm not a cop, and I know that there's not much I can do. However, your friend's death was my fault. You can't argue that. He wouldn't have been out there if it hadn't been for me. If you care about me at all, let me be a part of this. I won't be in the way." Her words flew faster and faster as she pleaded her case.

He definitely should have kept walking. When she spoke to him like that, and wore her heart on her sleeve, it pulled at him and it made him soften. He didn't like it. He let out a long sigh.

"I appreciate the offer—"

"Don't." She paused, like she was trying to find the right words to completely unlock him. "I need to do this, or I'm never going to be able to look at myself in the mirror. I can't sit by and watch you and your department struggle." She motioned toward the bullpen where the woman had been crying.

He walked back to his desk and opened up a drawer. He pulled out a waiver. "I can't have you along in any professional capacity, but you have the right as a private citizen to ride along with law enforcement. However, you have to sign this." He slid the paper across his desk and then tossed her a pen.

Her eyes brightened and a smile took over her features, making her even more beautiful and impossible to say no to than ever. This was gonna be one hell of an investigation if he had her tagging along, but he knew entirely too well how she was feeling and the weight that was bearing down on her soul. That same weight was bearing on his. They needed answers, and this was one time he hoped that having all hands on deck would lead to the answers everyone so desperately needed.

Chapter Nine

After having Penny call the rest of her patients for today as well as the rest of the week to reschedule, Holly left the clinic. It had been a gamble showing up in Ty's office and asking to be a part of this investigation. To be honest, she was a little surprised that Ty had agreed to let her come along with him, but she wasn't about to look a gift horse in the mouth. He must have sensed how seriously she needed to be involved.

Every time she had slowed down or stopped moving, she had found herself thinking about Moose and the way his head had nearly been completely cleaved from his body. Closing her eyes, she could still see the wet, red muscles and the creamy white and grayish exsanguinated flesh.

If Ty hadn't agreed to bring her along, he must have known that she would have been out there in the woods trying to figure out exactly what had happened to Moose. Though Ty seemed to like her, he didn't seem to like her enough to actually include her, so he must have heard the desperation and resolve in her voice and known what she would have done if he said no. She doubted he was acquiescing to her request out of some act of selflessness. He had probably just thought that letting her have some token role in this would keep her from going rogue. This was probably his attempt to keep her in check.

Regardless of his motivations, she was glad to have a place at the table.

After she had signed the waiver, he had planted her outside his office while he talked to several of the other officers. The assistant who'd shown her to the office was silently crying in the corner and one of her coworkers was sitting with her, whispering.

There was the occasional ring of the phones and clatter of typing, but the office was surprisingly quiet. She wondered if that was because of what had transpired or if this was typical. Her office had been livelier than this place.

She hadn't known what to expect when she'd arrived, but she had assumed that his active investigation would not include so much desk work or her twiddling her thumbs in a hard plastic seat outside his door. Yet, here she was. Perhaps, she had romanticized this just as much as she had once romanticized him.

Why is reality always so much less exciting than fantasy?

She tried to listen hard to hear Ty's voice from behind his closed door, however all she could make out was the occasional rumble of his voice.

After a while, the woman who'd brought her back here stopped crying. Puffy-eyed, she'd made her way back out to her workstation and her friend had moved back to her desk. Every few minutes, the friend would look over at her with curiosity. She looked to be in her early thirties, dark-haired and toned. Holly found herself wondering if the woman was the kind Ty would have dated.

No. He'd made it clear in his office that he wasn't the kind to date coworkers. He also was the kind who had clear feelings on the topic. As much as it annoyed her, she hated to admit that of course she felt the same way. There was just something about him being so judgmental with her that ticked her off.

The woman looked up from her computer and caught Holly looking at her. She stood up from her desk and grabbed a coffee cup that had a picture of a sheriff's badge emblazoned on it. Then she made her way over to the Keurig near the back wall. She hit the button and then, as the coffee maker kicked on, she walked over toward her. "Hey, how's it going?"

Holly smiled. "Good. Thanks."

"I'm Valerie Keller," the woman said, extending her hand in welcome.

"Holly," she said, shaking hands.

"Dean. Right?"

Of course, the woman knows my name, she thought, trying to cover her initial surprise at the woman's recognition of her. She had been at the center of yesterday's callout.

She nodded.

"I'm glad to see you are up and running today. I heard you'd been hurt."

Holly waved her off. "Nothing major. Skin glue and butterfly strips were all it needed—I didn't even bother going in to the hospital after I got a real look at it at home."

That being said, it was going to leave one heck of a nasty scar.

"We didn't get a chance to meet, but I was one of the SAR members up there looking for you. My team came in from the bottom of the hill." She smiled, brightly.

Holly didn't know exactly what it was, maybe it was the woman's warmth or the fact that she had tried to rescue her, but she liked her. The woman had a spark, and given the chance, she was sure they could be friends.

"Thank you," Holly said, returning Valerie's warm smile. "I'm sorry I had everyone so upset. It was never my intention."

Valerie shrugged. "Things happen. No one ever wants to be in a situation where they need us, and yet we have jobs for a reason." She touched her shoulder. "I'm glad we got to you in time."

"Me, too," Holly said, nodding as she tried to ignore the guilt in her belly. "I'm sorry about Moose."

"Yes. I appreciate that." The woman's smile faded, and she glanced toward the coffee maker. "Do you want a cup of coffee while you wait for Ty? He might be in there for a while. West had a list of things he wanted to talk about today."

"Did he work all day yesterday, too? You know, before he had the show up on the mountain?" She gave her a sheepish look.

Valerie nodded. "Yeah, but we are used to those kinds of hours. We knew exactly what we signed up for when we chose to join Search and Rescue. If anything, we should thank you for keeping our skills on point. Plus, I must admit that it is fun to get up there on the mountain."

She was surprised by the woman given how the day had turned out, but she was grateful for Valerie making light of the situation.

The woman walked back to the Keurig and grabbed a couple cups of coffee and handed her one. She took a sip and gave the woman a thankful tip of the head.

"By the way, do you work with Robert Finch?"

Holly nodded. "Why do you ask?"

Valerie shrugged nonchalantly. "Oh, he went on a few dates with my sister, Evelyn."

Of course, he did.

The woman stared at her, like she was looking for answers in her face. Holly tried to remain unreadable. "Are they still together?"

"My sister said things between them were really heating up. Yet, I think Robert was still seeing a couple other women. I don't know, though. You know how dating is now. I miss the good old days when people dated one person at a time, instead of dating twenty." She gave an annoyed chuckle.

"Oh, sister, I hear you." She glanced back at the closed door. "Robert is always dating somebody new, so I feel for your sister." She didn't want to tell her about Robert's incessant calling and texting, or how he had shown up at her house.

"I tried to warn her off him. I had heard about his reputation, but Evelyn swore that she loved him."

"But she knew Robert was a sleaze?" Holly didn't get it. She wasn't the kind of woman to put up with that kind of thing, or Robert for that matter.

Maybe that was why she was usually single.

Valerie shrugged. "I love her and act as her sounding board. Unfortunately, at the end of the day it doesn't matter what I think—it's her circus, her monkey."

It didn't escape her that the woman had compared Robert to a lesser ape. She glanced back over at Ty's door. While she didn't necessarily agree with the woman's condemnation when it came to all men, she had to chuckle. Besides, it wasn't like women were any better. People were merely *people*.

Ty's door cracked open, and the other officer came

walking out. He had a stony expression on his face, as though he had just gotten in trouble. Ty stepped out behind him, watching the guy as he walked away. He disappeared back into his office for a moment before reappearing with his jacket thrown over his arm.

He looked over at her. "You ready?" he asked, like he had been the one waiting for her and not the other way around.

Valerie gave her a tip of the head. "Good luck with him. He looks like he's in a mood," she whispered. "Watch out…when he's like this, he bites."

She could handle the occasional nibble, especially in bed, but she wasn't about to allow herself to get bitten by him.

She stood up and touched Valerie's arm appreciatively before turning away and looking to Ty. "I'm ready whenever you are."

He rushed past her, barely waiting for her in his hurry to leave the office. Based on his coworker's expression and his behavior, whatever had occurred behind that closed door had been unpleasant.

By the time they made it to his pickup, his gait had slowed from nearly a sprint to a simple march. She made sure to stay three steps behind and safely out of proximity of his teeth.

He opened his department-issued truck's door for her, and she hesitated to get in with him, but he was staring out into the rest of the parking lot and didn't seem to notice.

As he closed the door and walked around to the other side of the pickup, she wasn't sure what she could do or say in order to help him. She also wasn't sure if she should ask where they were going, or what he planned to do. Then again, it really didn't matter. She was here legally, as a bystander and nothing more.

While she was happy to at least have some active role in the investigation, she wished there was something more she could do to make a difference besides being a passenger princess to the snarling beast.

As he roared out of the parking lot and onto the main road, she waited for him to say something.

Was he mad at her? Or, was this solely about something that had been said in his meeting?

She waited, going down the swirling funnel of self-deprecating and questioning thoughts. Finally, just as they were about to get on the snowy road that led toward Bozeman he spoke up. "Are you hungry?"

Of all the things she thought he would say to reestablish communications between them, that had been near the bottom of the list. Or, maybe he was hangry and that was what was really bothering him.

"No, but I can always go for a cup of coffee or something, if you are."

He grumbled something under his breath.

"Look, if you are going to act like a feral animal the entire time we are together, you need to let me ride in the back of the pickup or something."

He opened his mouth like he was about to argue with her, but then clamped his mouth shut for a second. The tension sat in the air between them like a ticking time bomb. "Sorry," he clipped.

"No, you're not." She was poking the bear, but she didn't care. She didn't want false platitudes—what she wanted was honesty.

"You're right. I'm not sorry. I'm furious. I don't know why you couldn't just tell me the truth."

What? How could he be mad at me?

"What did I do?" she asked, completely bewildered that she was the cause of his problematic behavior.

"I heard all about your relationship with Robert. I thought you said you weren't dating him, and he wasn't your boyfriend." He stared over at her like he was tempted to stop the truck and make her get out.

She was tempted to, as it was. "I didn't have a relationship with Robert. I don't know how many times I have to tell you that. And I sure as hell don't know where you heard such outrageous lies."

"My buddy back there," he said, jabbing his thumb in the direction they'd come from, "said he is good friends with your *friend* Robert. He let me know Robert had been...what'd he call it?" He sneered. "*Bagging you* for at least the last six months."

Oh, for the love of all... Is he kidding me?

She nearly growled. "Robert has a big mouth."

Ty slowed the truck down, but only slightly. "So, you did sleep with him?"

"That's not even remotely close to what I said. Robert makes moves on any woman who even pays attention to him. If I had to guess, he is probably clinically a sex addict. I told you before, and I wish you'd respect me enough to believe me, but I wouldn't have a relationship with that man if he was the last person on earth."

"Has anything physical ever transpired between the two of you?" He pressed one more time.

"Detective Terrell, I do not require interrogation and I stand by my previous statement. If you continue to interrogate me, I will work on Moose's death investigation by myself." She reached down and put her hand on the door handle like she was tempted to tuck and roll out of the moving vehicle.

Ty sighed. "Okay. Okay." He ran his hand over his face like he was trying to wipe his mind clear of the thoughts about her.

She hadn't lied, but she certainly wasn't about to tell him that Robert had drunkenly kissed her at last year's Halloween costume party, or anything else. It was none of Ty's business and it held no bearing on their time together.

"Why is it so important to know about my past? What does Robert have to do with the investigation we're conducting?" she countered, meeting fire with fire once again.

This, this hard-headedness and refusal to back down, was why they could never be together. That, and a myriad of other reasons.

Ty sighed again. "It doesn't... I just..." He gripped the wheel tight. "West only brought it up because he saw you outside my office. He recognized you. Apparently, Robert had been showing him pictures of the two of you together. I shouldn't have let it get under my skin."

"First, I don't know why there would have been pictures, unless they are ones for our practice. Second, what else did West tell you? I'll be more than happy to clear things up with Robert as soon as I see him. He has no right to talk about me or spread malicious lies about things that never occurred. In fact—" she paused, realizing that now she was the one snarling "—I'm going to do my damnedest to make sure that he doesn't have a job."

That seemed to temper Ty's rage. Though, she was still at a loss as to why he would have been so upset. Even if she had been sleeping with Robert, it didn't have any bearing on what she and Ty were doing, and he had no reason to be covetous of her.

"I know that I have no right to have a say in who you choose or have chosen to date. But I think you can do better than Robert."

She wanted to ask if he had someone better in mind, but she held her tongue. "In that, you won't find an argument with me."

Especially when the man she really wanted was the one at her side.

Chapter Ten

Ty had been given the choice to attend Moose's autopsy or step aside and allow another detective to be present during the investigation. The thought of being there bothered him, but so did the idea of passing the duty on to someone else who knew Moose. There was only one right way to handle this—he had a duty and role in which to honor his friend.

He glanced over at Holly, who kept making her way right back into his life and into the thick of things. He couldn't deny her anything. As much as he didn't want to, he cared about her too much to ignore her feelings. She wanted to be a part of this, and he could understand why. Although she couldn't have possibly understood what she had just signed up for and how much it would cost her in the long run.

No matter what, he couldn't allow her to join him in the autopsy suite. There were things no one needed to witness unless they were required.

As it was, he was going to have to dissociate like never before when he stepped foot in there. And, though it wasn't something he could admit out loud, he was actually glad that Holly would be there waiting for him when he stepped out of those doors and away from his friend's remains.

As they neared a drive-through coffee shop on the edge of town, he slowed down and pulled in. He didn't need anything, but he also wasn't in a hurry to get to the state crime lab in Billings and the office where they were going to be performing the autopsy.

"What kind of coffee would you like?" he asked Holly, turning to face her.

"You guys really have a thing for coffee, don't you?" she said with a little smile.

He didn't understand her joke. "You mean cops? You know it. We work wonky hours and it helps—we drink a lot of energy drinks, too."

He pulled up to the window to order. "I'll take a blue energy drink, extra cream. You?"

Holly looked at the menu before ordering a plain black coffee. He added on a couple blueberry muffins for good measure.

There was a white pickup that slowly drove by. It had been behind them now for about the last five miles. He glanced over at the truck, but as it creeped past, he couldn't see the driver inside. A knot clenched in his gut, though he couldn't have said why.

The girl at the window said their total, but he barely heard her as he handed her a twenty and took their drinks and food. He didn't stop staring at the truck. It was a King Ranch pickup. He had seen one like it before in town— outside Holly's place.

He thought about asking Holly if she thought Robert would be following them, but he changed his mind. He'd promised her that he would leave any talk about that guy at the door.

He'd grilled her enough.

It was just that Detective West had been adamant

that the guy was sleeping with Holly and in a current relationship. He needed to take her word and trust her that nothing had ever happened between her and Robert. Trust, however, had never been his strong suit. He was too deeply embroiled in the world of secrets to think that anyone was above lies and using crime to get ahead.

He was making something out of nothing, and his mind was playing tricks on him. Moreover, he was on edge thanks to everything that had been going on in his life in the last day or two. He needed to relax.

He moved his truck forward just enough to get out of the way of the people behind him in line, but he pretended to pick at his muffin as he watched the King Ranch pickup turn down the road ahead of them.

"Are you okay?" Holly asked, taking a sip of her coffee.

"Hmm?" he said, glancing over at her, trying to reassure himself that some psychopath wasn't following them. If she didn't notice Robert's pickup, then it had to mean he wasn't a threat and Ty was making something of nothing. "Yeah, why do you ask?" he asked, trying to play off his behavior.

"I don't want you to be upset with me," she started, seemingly unaware of the war he was raging with his intuition. "If we are going to work together, or at least I'm going to be your sidekick or whatever, we need to get along."

Of course, she thinks this is about her...

He couldn't explain it, or help her to understand, that his gut was telling him something was more than just off with Robert. And no matter what—and what he wanted more than anything—was to make sure she was safe and well protected. Especially when it came to the man who had been banging on her door.

He would never trust that man.

"Are you going to answer me?" she asked, pulling him from his condemnations.

"I agree. Sorry, I'm out of sorts. It's been a long day. I'm sure you get it. And I'm sorry about the way I've been acting. It's not you, it's me." He heard his last words fall flat in the air. They harkened back to another time and place he didn't want to bring up with her.

"I…" She paused, like she was thinking something close to what he was. "I appreciate your apologies. Let's just start over. Really. Let's leave some hatchets buried."

Yep. We are definitely on the same page there.

"So," she continued, "where is it that you are taking me?"

He'd been so wrapped up in his thoughts that he realized how accommodating she had been with his silence. He put his drink in the cupholder and his muffin on the dashboard before easing his way out onto the main road again. "We need to run to Billings. They are rushing Moose's autopsy and I have to be present."

"Autopsy?" she said the word painfully slow.

"Don't worry about it, you are just going to wait outside." He smiled in his attempt to console her.

She nodded.

As they turned to go toward the highway, there was a *plink* sound. He couldn't quite put his finger on it. There was another, *plink*.

A spiderweb of cracks moved through his windshield around a tiny hole at their epicenter.

"Get down!" he yelled, reaching over and pushing Holly's head down and toward the floor for cover. "He's shooting at us!"

There was the *plink* again as another round struck the glass near where his head had been only moments before.

He slowed down and grabbed his radio, reaching out to 911 as he flipped on his concealed red and blue lights and sirens. "Shots fired. Shots fired. Near the corner of 34th and Main. Send all available deputies."

There was the crackle of the radio and the 911 dispatcher's response. Units were on the way.

He reached behind his seat and pulled out his rifle, slapping the magazine to make sure it was seated. "Don't move. Stay low and behind cover. I don't want you getting hurt. You understand me?" He stared at Holly, who looked wide-eyed with terror.

"Who is shooting at us?"

He shrugged, but he had a feeling he knew exactly who was pulling the trigger—and who was about to go down in a blaze of gunfire.

He always wore his tactical vest under his uniform shirt when he was in the office. Today was one of those days he was glad he went overboard with caution. As a detective, he rarely found himself on the wrong end of a gun, but today just happened to be one of those days.

The sirens blared around them, hopefully doing their job to disorient the shooter or at least pull some of their focus away from their intended target—who was, in this case, him.

He got low, but gunned the gas and raced his truck in the direction of the shooter. They had to neutralize the threat before the shooter grew bolder or started to shoot at innocent bystanders.

In front of him, from inside the white pickup that had been following them, a person—who he assumed was Robert—was pointing a gun in their direction. *Plink*.

The guy is shooting suppressed.

The silencer was doing its job, but the muffled gunfire made chills run down his spine.

He pressed the gas harder, all the way to the floor, as he accelerated toward the shooter. One of them was going to die, and he doubted it would be him.

Ping.

Another round hit his truck and threw shrapnel on impact. There didn't appear to be any bystanders in his line of sight, but there was definitely the coffee shop girl and who knew who else inside one of the buildings near them. Robert wasn't going to stop until he killed someone.

He placed his gun by his leg, grabbed at the radio and flicked on the intercom. "Put down your weapon! If you do not put down your weapon, we will shoot!"

As he took the corner, his tires screeched on the asphalt and kicked up gravel.

The driver took off, but they were faster. He rammed his pickup into the corner of the guy's truck with a smash. Holly lurched forward in her seat, and he started to reach over, instinctively to catch her, but his rifle was still in his hand and he was forced to just hold on.

Damn it. This isn't good.

He couldn't get in a hot pursuit like this with her in the car. He couldn't put her in more danger.

However, he couldn't let the guy go. He was a risk to public safety.

The guy gained control over his fishtailing rig, and he laid the pedal down. He tore off, and Ty let him gain some distance. Robert's truck was heavier than his, but if he had the chance he would ram him again. Next time, into something that could help to stop him. If he stayed on the highway, there was a line of concrete medians that could act as rams.

He called in to dispatch. "Let's get another unit ready to throw spike strips two miles out." He gave them the mile marker where they could safely neutralize the vehicle.

There were a few junctions before that point, but if Robert stayed on the highway they needed to get him stopped.

He kept a wary eye on the driver, who was constantly checking his mirrors and looking back, watching them. From where they were, he couldn't make out Robert's face for a clear identification. The driver was wearing a baseball hat and sunglasses. He was nearly positive it was Robert, but he wasn't entirely sure.

Who else could it have been? As far as he knew, that was the only person who wanted him dead—or, who wanted Holly taken out.

He'd been hoping that Robert had just had too much to drink last night. As it was, the guy was acting like he was completely out of control.

"Is Robert's behavior...this disregard for safety and focus on you, normal?" he asked, looking at Holly, who had righted herself in her seat but was still carefully hunched below the windows.

She shook her head. "He definitely watches over me. I'd say he's even overprotective."

"Do you know if he has had any history of mental illness or breakdowns?"

She shook her head. "He has always been...not like this, but...*different*. Kind of like an extreme frat guy who didn't completely grow up. You know?"

He put his rifle down by his leg and opened up his

computer and tapped away as he also tried to keep an eye on the road. "It doesn't look like he has any prior arrests."

No matter what the computer said, Robert should have been arrested for something by now. He didn't seem like the kind of guy who played by the rules.

The pickup veered hard to the right, down a logging road that went deep into the mountains. The road connected with at least a dozen more.

Ah, hell.

From them, he could end up anywhere from Bozeman to Wyoming.

He couldn't go on this pursuit all by himself. There was no way he could safely do this until he had more backup. On those icy mountain roads, almost as soon as a person got off the highway, they lost cell phone reception.

He carefully typed a message to dispatch on his as he drove. The other units were about twenty minutes out. Until they reached him, he decided to stay put and come up with a game plan.

He slowed his truck down and pulled to the side of the road.

"What are you doing?" Holly asked, sounding alarmed. "We can't let him go!"

He nudged his chin in the direction the truck and its driver had disappeared. "He won't hurt anyone but himself up in those mountains. Until I have more manpower, I'm not going in. And I'm not putting you at risk."

"You're putting me at risk by not stopping him now." She sounded angry as she sat up. "He just *shot* at us. You can't let him drive away."

"Who said I was going to let him get away?" he countered, though he could understand from her perspective why she would be so upset.

He was amped and ready to keep going, but he couldn't go full throttle. He had teams, teams of people who were trained for these types of pursuits. And frankly, since becoming a detective, he was not as up to date as his junior team members on tactics employed in a high-speed chase. At the top of his game, when he'd been on patrol, he doubted that the suspect would have slipped through his fingers when he'd attempted the pit maneuver.

The more he thought about how he'd failed, the angrier he became. He should have shot at the suspect. Screw trying to neutralize the vehicle.

As he put the truck in Park, he ran his hand over his face. No doubt this was going to be armchair quarterbacked and picked apart by everyone else who hadn't been on scene and making the tough calls.

The one thing he was better at, and more experienced with, was thinking outside the box. The younger patrolman could chase the driver through the woods. He could find Robert another way. He would simply have to outsmart the man who was so intent on killing.

Chapter Eleven

Holly was furious. She just couldn't believe that Ty had simply given up the chase. In fact, he'd even seemed almost relieved when three other squad cars showed up, along with a Forest Service ranger and an on-duty game warden who wanted to help with the chase. She couldn't believe that the only person who didn't want to go after this guy was Ty. It didn't make sense.

She was so mad she could have almost spit.

He was out talking to the game warden now, some guy named Aaron. She appreciated that he was being chummy, but talking wasn't bringing their attacker to heel.

What doesn't Ty understand? He knows this guy is trying to kill me, but he is too busy talking to do what has to be done.

She looked over at the steering wheel and the set of keys that were dangling from the ignition of his pickup. The lady on the radio for dispatch broke the tense silence inside the cab. "Reports of a white King Ranch being seen on forest road 17890, headed west."

She continued, but Holly's attention was diverted by the two patrol units, SUVs, that pulled around them and onto the dirt road and headed toward the mountain and what must have been the named road. One of the deputies who had taken the call said something over the radio to dispatch.

Two other deputies had already headed out. Ty and Aaron just stood there, talking.

She looked at the keys again. Maybe she could just start the truck and get his attention and gently remind him she was chomping at the bit.

As if he could sense her frustration he turned and looked at her. She put her hands up, trying not to be too much, but still getting her question of what was going on across. He gave her a thumbs-up.

She couldn't stand it; she reached over and started the pickup, hoping that it would act as some sign that she was waiting impatiently. Ty looked surprised as he glanced over at her and the running pickup. She didn't know how much clearer she could be. He said something to the game warden, and slowly approached the pickup. He walked around to the driver's-side door and opened it, looked at her. "What do you think you're doing?"

She'd screwed up.

Her impatience had won out over her logical thinking. Why did she have to be that way sometimes?

"Sorry, I was getting cold, I didn't mean to bother you." She tried to cover up her mistake.

He glanced at her warm winter clothing but nodded. "You're fine." He climbed into his seat. "I'm sorry that took a little bit—I am trying to get everybody lined up and in place. So far, none of our guys have spotted him, but a civilian just called in with a possible sighting."

She nodded, thinking about what she'd heard over the radio.

"But I did get the search warrant filed with the judge."

"Search warrant? For what?" She felt horrible for having been impatient.

"While my crew is looking for Robert up here, I am going to see if we can find anything of interest in his residence."

"What do you mean anything of interest?" Holly asked. "What are you hoping to find?"

"I think based on his behavior, that Robert may have either significant mental health issues or a drug problem. Do you think it's possible that he's been running drugs out of your clinic?" He shot her a glance, and it made her wonder if he somehow questioned whether or not she would have been involved in something as ethically and legally questionable as what he was assuming Robert was capable of.

"We don't overlap on patients, and I don't review his work, so I guess it's possible. However, he hasn't acted like this before and he hasn't been this erratic, so I'm not sure what is going on."

He sighed.

She could understand his frustration, she was feeling that way, as well. At least his life wasn't the one on the line. Well, that wasn't exactly true, Robert had been shooting at him, too. Part of her wanted to tell him to take her home, but at the same time she was probably better protected with Ty by her side. Not to mention the fact that there was something about being with Ty. Heck, he couldn't even leave her in the truck while he spoke with the game warden without her getting impatient and needing him closer.

It was quiet in the truck as Ty got them going on the logging road. He dialed the phone and held it between his shoulder and cheek. She could hear someone answer on the other side. "Hi, Doctor Schultz, I was hoping to get a report on George Dolack's autopsy. I'm sorry I couldn't be there, however we had an incident arise and I needed to stay close to Big Sky."

The medical examiner said something in the background that she couldn't quite hear. As the man spoke, Ty's expression darkened, and he gripped the wheel hard.

"Can you go ahead and send me your report when you get it written?" he asked.

There was a heaviness in his voice that made Holly wonder what the examiner had told him. It clearly wasn't good, but nothing about this situation had been thus far so she didn't know how she could expect anything different.

They spoke for a few more minutes. She watched out the window as the snow-covered timber flashed by her window while they made their way out of the woods and back toward town. As they neared the intersection where the shots had been fired, she felt her body stiffen.

He slowed down by the little coffee shop. There was a series of spray paint marks where they had been parked and where the shooter had been.

She shouldn't have been surprised, but she was slightly taken aback that so much had been investigated already at the scene of the shooting. More than anything, what shocked her was that other patrol officers had already been there and left in the time that they had been on the mountain. It didn't feel like they had been gone that long.

The shooting had been such a canon event for her, and yet the on-scene investigation had only taken a few hours. It was amazing to think that they were already done and had aggregated their findings. Then again, they were there just collecting information—not passing judgments. As such, there was little gray area when it came to the actual physical evidence.

Once they had parked back at the station, she got out and took a peek at the truck. There were four bullet holes, one in the glass where Ty had been sitting. Oddly enough, it was the only one that had been close to hitting either one of them. Either Robert was a terrible shot, or he hadn't really been trying to kill them. She had to lean toward him being a horrible marksman.

Ty hung up the phone and stepped out of the pickup. He was gritting his teeth and the color had leached from his face as he took a series of pictures of the damage to his work truck. He sent the pictures off on email to his evidence techs. She wasn't sure what to do, or if she should try to get him to talk or to let him stew in silence until he was ready. Maybe she could extend her hand. She yearned to console him.

As though he could sense her feelings, he held out his hand, palm up expectantly. As she looked at his hand, he nudged his chin toward his fingers, like he was trying to persuade a gentle horse to do his bidding. She wasn't the kind of woman to be told what to do, and yet she found herself reaching over and slipping her hand into his. He wrapped his fingers around hers and finally sent her a small smile.

He grazed the back of her hand gently with his callused thumb.

There was a sickening lump in her stomach as she thought about how close they had come to being killed. She glanced at the bullet hole in the driver's-side windshield, mere inches from where Ty had been sitting. She grabbed his hand harder. "I'm sorry."

"What are you sorry about? You've done nothing

wrong." Ty turned and gave her that sexy half smile that had a way of making her feel safe.

"I'm sorry for bringing all this into your life."

"You don't need to apologize anymore. This chaos, this constant edge of the seat living, that *is* my life."

"You can't tell me that you're getting shot at every day, or that your friends get killed." She instantly regretted saying the last bit.

Why did she have to keep circling back to things that brought Ty pain? It was like she just kept having to put more salt in his wounds.

"No, but there's always something. My life is never really easy. I'm always busy. I'm always involved in some sort of investigation or sex crime or death."

She stood in silence, unsure how to respond other than to simply let him speak. She wondered if he ever just talked about the things he faced.

Though she understood the emotional upheaval that likely came with being in law enforcement, she hadn't thought about the drain it must have placed on him. Of course, things like this were part of his daily life and it threw a harsh light on her own blessed experience.

For her, an exciting day meant that one of her patients had done their exercises as prescribed and were seeing her pain-free; that was what it meant to do a good job or have a job well done. For him, a job well-done meant that he put all the pieces of a death together, or any crime, and made sense of a myriad of perspectives and stories until a condensed version of the truth was exposed.

"For now, I'm going to leave my work truck here so the evidence team can go over it with a fine-tooth comb. I hope you are okay with riding in style." He motioned toward the employee lot where a late-model Dodge Ram pickup was parked. "It ain't fancy, but she is mine."

She smiled, but the action was forced. She didn't mind riding in his pickup, just so long as she was able to continue working by his side. "I don't care about fancy…as long as we are safe and can get some answers."

He nodded, but his face became stern. "Yeah… Did I tell you the medical examiner said that Moose also had a puncture wound to his chest? He said it was consistent with likely being caused by a large knife."

She stopped walking and stood in shocked silence for a long moment. Ty kept walking, but after a moment he turned and came back for her.

"What? But on the mountain…no one had mentioned any wounds besides that on his neck."

"The coroner must have missed it. There had been a ton of blood and Moose had been wearing heavy layers. It's not unusual for the initial findings to be incomplete under those types of conditions." He slipped his hand in hers and helped her toward his pickup and then inside.

She sat staring out the window, half expecting to see the hole and cracking where a bullet had shattered the glass, but she found it complete and unmarked. Someone out there was determined to commit murder—they had completed their job once—what was stopping them from killing them? Or, what if there was more than one killer?

Ty climbed into the pickup and started the engine.

"His death was clearly no accident." She had thought it was possible that he'd been murdered, but she had held out a sliver of hope that it was nothing more than a tragic accident, but that hope had been dashed. "Who was on that mountain that would have wanted him dead?"

Ty shook his head. "I looked at the pictures we took

up on the hillside, but it was hard to see anything too distinctive. There weren't any good foot tracks, but the footprints that were in the snow that weren't his were slightly smaller. They were wearing snow boots, but beyond that I have no idea as to who was wearing them."

Holly pursed her lips. "That's not a bad place to start. Whoever murdered him must likely have been shorter and smaller than him. How tall was Moose?"

Ty shrugged. "He was taller than me, but not by much so I think he was probably about six foot two."

"So, he probably wore about a size twelve and a half shoe?" There weren't a whole lot of people she could think of around town who were taller or bigger than what he was describing, but this kind of thinking made her feel as though she was grasping at straws.

"Whoever did it could have been someone he knew, making it easier to get access to him. What I can't make sense of is who had access like that and why they'd risk murdering him in such a remote area? There had to be other times and places they could have killed him that would have been easier." Ty tapped on the wheel. "I just don't get it."

"Do you have a list of the SAR members who were out on the slopes that day?"

Ty nodded. "Of course, but there were only handful people and all of them were accounted for. No one was alone, they were working in pairs. The only person who was trying to lone wolf besides me was Moose."

"Have you talked to everyone?" she asked.

"I talked to most of the team. We've all been texting after what happened."

"But you didn't talk to any of them in person?" she countered.

"We have a scheduled debriefing tonight, but with everything happening…"

"I think you should make sure that happens. Even if they were accompanied at all times, maybe one of them saw something who could help us figure out what happened up there on the hill."

He sighed, as though he had already been thinking that and she was simply voicing his plans. She should just shut her mouth. He was the detective, and she was only along for the ride. She had to remember her place—or did she?

"I'll talk to them, too."

He nodded. "Sure, but let's work this thing together."

His reaction surprised her. It was a funny thing, sometimes she found that her worst enemies were her thoughts. The only thing holding her back was herself and her assumptions.

She squeezed Ty's hand, grateful that he couldn't hear the things that she was thinking. She didn't want him to know the battles she fought within herself, about not only her way of thinking but also about how she felt about him.

It would be a lie if she told herself that she didn't have feelings for him and that they hadn't been reawakened during this time together. She wanted him in ways she hadn't wanted a man in a long time. She wanted him to take her, to own her.

However, the desire to be owned didn't sit right with her. Men and women were to stand side by side, not to have a man in front and to take control. Then again, there were times when that was exactly what she wanted and she hated it. Perhaps what she hated most was that there was no strict duality in her thoughts and feelings. Maybe what she really wanted was for things to be easy; and for them to have the simple love and feelings that had been at the pinnacle of their youth.

It would be unreasonable to think that they could ever go back to those days and that kind of love. It was also important that she didn't get stuck in the recursive loop of yearning for moments in time and life that had slipped from her grasp like dust motes. All she could do now was to grasp the moments she had as they fluttered by and live them as fully and as greatly as she was capable.

Before she realized, they were parked in front of the chestnut-brown seventies-style house she recognized as Robert's. Ty let go of her hand and opened up his computer and tapped away at his emails. Her skin cooled from where his hand had been pressed against hers. She wanted him...more than just his hand in hers, more than just a simple touch. She wanted *all* of him.

"Did you get what you needed?" she asked, aware that she wasn't only asking about a search warrant or some email.

He looked up at her, as though he had heard something else in her question, as well. "The judge has it now. I think the search warrant will be signed within the next ten minutes or so. In the meantime, we will wait here in case Robert shows back up. We also have other units coming in from DCI to act in a supporting role in this case. You know, all hands on deck."

He looked resignedly at the computer screen like he was willing the judge to come through.

"Do you need to wait until another unit gets here or can you go in without them?" she asked, having no idea what kind of protocols he was supposed to adhere to.

He looked over at her with a slight grin and it made her want to lean over and kiss him. "Nothing about this case has been normal. In fact, there have only been a handful of cases in which we've even needed to call in other counties for partnership assists. I'm sure that the sheriff has been on the phone with DCI all morning, too."

"DCI?"

"It's the division of criminal investigation from the state DOJ. They are out of Helena, and they are the oversight unit that works across the state. In our case, the sheriff will likely request that they come in and handle the entire case as an oversight since we are using resources from multiple counties. It's just another way to create a hierarchy and accountability—especially since Moose was one of our own."

She nodded, understanding why a unit like theirs would be necessary, though she hadn't heard about them before. There was so much that Ty did that she'd never realized and she continually found herself humbled.

"So, in essence, you will be accountable to them?"

He nodded, slightly. "Yes, but I'm not concerned. I'm always accountable to a myriad of people for every choice and action I take. There's a lot resting on my shoulders."

His statement made something inside her shift. He really was an incredible man. He bore so much and was currently facing what had to be one of his largest crises yet, not to mention the personal toll of losing his friend, and he was handling it all with a level of professionalism and aplomb that was truly commendable.

"I wish we had gotten Robert back there on the road. It would have made my job easier. At least I could concentrate on Moose's death. I don't know what it is about this job, but it seems like any time something big happens, something bigger comes along. It's never one thing at a time."

Now that was a feeling she could relate to. "That's how it is at the clinic, too. If there's an emergency, then there is at least one more in the same hour."

She snorted as she thought about the last time it had happened a few months ago, when a man had come in with excruciating back pain and they had found out it wasn't stemming from his back and instead he was suffering from a heart attack. At the same time, a woman came in with neck pain and they realized she had, in fact, broken a vertebra and was lucky not to be paralyzed. Both people had to be sent by ambulance to the emergency room in Bozeman.

The EMS workers had even asked them if they were going to send another and, if they were, if they could just pick them up at the same time in order to save themselves a trip—they had really thought themselves funny.

Luckily, both of her patients had survived and come through their traumatic events.

He moved his computer out of the way and leaned closer to her. "You know...while we have a second..." His gaze met hers and she found herself only thinking about the depths of the darkness at the center of his.

"Yes?" she asked, her voice far breathier than she had intended.

He smiled brightly. "You know...when we get this all sorted out, I'd love to take you on a real date. One that doesn't include search warrants or autopsy reports."

She couldn't help but laugh. "Why do I get the feeling that such a thing would be asking for a lot?"

He reached over and took her hand again. "It would be, but for you...it would be worth it." He lifted their entwined fingers and gave her a gentle kiss to the back of her knuckles.

The unexpected kiss and the warmth of his mouth made her gasp. Her body clenched and she felt a warmth rise up from between her thighs.

He couldn't have known what he was doing to her or what he was making her feel. It wasn't fair to tease her like this…to make her want and fantasize about him doing things to her that were not going to happen.

He looked up at her again and smiled. Reaching over with his free hand, he cupped her face and drew her mouth to his. He tasted of peppermint gum as her tongue grazed his lip. As their kiss deepened, she found that her own urgency was matched by his.

He wanted her.

He wanted her just like she wanted him.

She ached as she opened her legs wide, willing him to find his way between them.

He leaned back, breaking their kiss as he looked down and saw her body waiting to receive him. He smiled widely. Her gaze moved down him, and she found that he was wanting her just as much. Her mouth watered as she looked at how hard he pressed against his pants and down his thigh.

Some things about the past and their relationship she had forgotten, but how much he brought to the bed wasn't one of them.

"Ty…" She said his name like it was a moan. "Do you know how much I missed you?"

He nodded. "Probably half as much as I missed you, Holly."

Suddenly, there was the roar of a pickup and Ty dropped his hand from her face as he jerked his attention toward the sound.

Pulling up behind him was a black Tahoe.

He sighed. "It looks like we have company."

She touched the wetness on her lips. She didn't care about company. What she cared about was Ty and what they had just started and would hopefully, someday, get to finish.

Chapter Twelve

Ty may have made a mistake in kissing her. However, he just wasn't able to control himself. He'd had to devour those lips, to taste the sweetness on them and revel in the scent of her skin. She had smelled so good, something floral, but he hadn't been able to tell if it was from her perfume or her hair. Whatever it was, he wanted to take it deep into his lungs once again.

He hadn't got nearly enough of her, or gone to the depths of the places he'd needed and wanted to explore.

He needed to taste more of her, to lick every last drop of sweet sweat from her skin as he kissed down from her lips...

He stirred.

No, he reminded himself. *I definitely made a mistake.*

Not only was she somewhat the cause of his friend's death, but she was also part of an active investigation. There were so many ethically gray areas in his falling for her again that he simply couldn't take things between them any further.

The sensible part of him was relieved that the detective from DCI had pulled up behind them, ending things. If he got the opportunity to continue things with Holly tonight, or some other time, he wasn't sure what he would do. It would take a will of steel not to pull her back into his arms and show her all the things he'd missed doing to her over the years. He had thought of her so many times.

He had thought he had put all of those old feelings away; however now that he was facing her head-on and being in such close proximity, everything had just come back in waves.

He got out of his pickup, casting one more gaze in her direction as he berated himself. She looked as torn and confused as he was feeling. He took a little bit of delight in seeing that her reaction was much like his own.

"Why don't you wait here for a moment, and let me talk to this detective?"

Holly nodded, but she refused to meet his gaze.

Ty closed the door and walked back toward the waiting detective from DCI. He'd never been overly friendly with Detective Josh Stowe. They had worked together a few times before, and the man was all business and a bit too tall in the saddle for his liking.

The guy was tapping on his phone as Ty walked up. He rolled his window down. "How's it going, Stowe? I appreciate you coming our way. I'm sure you had a thousand other things on your plate today."

Stowe waved him off. "It's nice to get out of the office once in a while and deal with something fresh. I have a stack of cases on my desk I've been working on for months. Sometimes, it doesn't feel like they are going anywhere."

He could understand the feeling. "I hear you."

Stowe slapped the bottom of the window frame as he opened up the door and stepped outside. "I just talked to Sheriff Sanderson and had him give me a status report.

And I called the judge. He approved our warrant. Who all's going to be working this with us from your team?"

He just knew Stowe was going to love his answer. "Just you and me."

"That's it?" Stowe looked at his pickup. "Not the officer with you, as well?"

Of course, he'd assume anyone with Ty was a LEO, it wasn't a common thing to have a detective with company. That was more of a patrol officer thing, to have a ride along.

"She's a witness and she knows our suspect. In fact, it is my belief that she is the reason he's gone off the rails."

The other detective nodded, as if this was something he had seen a ton of times. "Relationships, man. It's a wonder that any of us make it out alive." Stowe laughed.

"You're not wrong." He leaned against the back of the truck and took out his phone to look at his emails. The judge had signed off on the search warrant; he wasn't surprised, but he wondered how the other detective knew before he had. Clearly, he must have made phone calls before he'd arrived on the scene. "As I'm sure you know we've already been here doing some surveillance. So far, we haven't seen anything to indicate that our suspect is inside the residence, but enough time has passed since the shooting we believe he may have been able to deposit any weapons he may have used inside. As for his pattern of life, normally during this time of day he is at work. Today, however, that obviously isn't the case."

"What are we looking for inside the home?"

He looked in the direction of the chestnut-brown house. The driveway had been shoveled during the last snowfall; berms of icy snow were stacked on each side. The sidewalk to the front door, however, was still littered with ice and patches of snow. Clearly, the guy wasn't having a lot of guests, at least through the front door.

"Due to the nature of the shooting, we are to collect any firearms, reloading supplies, surplus ammo, bullets, magazines, or any gun-related items. We're gonna need to test them to see if they were involved in the shooting in any way."

Stowe dipped his head in acknowledgment. "I know I told you in text, but I want to reiterate how sorry I am about your friend's passing. Have you made any headway on that case?"

Ty wasn't sure how the detective had gotten from their search warrant to Moose's death so quickly, but he appreciated the guy's sentiment—it was always hard to lose a fellow brother in blue, even if a person wasn't close to them. No doubt, for Stowe, Moose's death acted as a reminder that their job brought continual danger and unknown threats.

"Nothing so far. Just got the ME's autopsy report back. Looks like he suffered trauma consistent with that made by an eight-inch-long blade."

"That's a big knife." Stowe's expression darkened.

"That's what I thought, too. Larger than a folding knife carried by most hunters or outdoorsman. It's strange, but then again everything about his death was."

"That's kind of what I'd heard." Stowe scowled. "He was a good dude, though. Funny as hell."

"I miss him already."

"As I'm sure his girlfriends do," Stowe said, with a laugh. He glanced over at him like he was checking to make sure that his joke hadn't been too soon.

Ty chuckled, trying to pacify the guy. "Moose definitely had a harem. I haven't heard from any of them.

He'd been talking about settling down the last time we chatted, but who knows with him."

Stowe stared over at the house. "Do you think that any of them had anything to do with his death?"

Ty shrugged. "I can't see how. The only women on the hill, at least that I know about, were Valerie, Cindy and our vic. None of them reported having a relationship beyond friendship with him."

"What about the guys?"

Ty frowned. "I don't think Moose was dating any of them, either."

"That's not really what I meant, but that's also worth looking into."

Ty shrugged. "Not a whole lot surprises me anymore. You know how it is, you see everything."

"You think we are going to see anything interesting in this place? Anything unexpected?" Stowe asked, nudging his chin in the direction of Robert's house.

Ty stopped leaning and pressed down his shirt, nervously. He had no idea what they were walking into, but he was hoping that it would lead to some kind of answer and at least a resolution in this case. Holly needed to be kept safe and protected and out of the sites of that man.

"There's only one way to find out. Let's grab our gear and head over there." He walked to the back door of his truck, behind Holly and took out his kit.

Holly looked over her shoulder at him. Her blond hair was falling loose over her shoulders, and it caught the sun, making a halo effect around her face. He tried to control the thrashing in his chest as he looked at her. She was so goddamn beautiful that she could nearly make him forget everything else that was going on in their world.

All he wanted to do was kiss her again—mistake or no

mistake, at least for those precious seconds he was exactly where he wanted to be and doing exactly what he wanted to do. Kissing her was where he belonged.

She ran her hand over her face, pushing a wayward hair behind her ear, nervously. "Can I come with you? I promise I won't touch anything. I just don't want to be sitting out here, all alone."

Her voice was high-pitched and airy, and he could hear her fear and it felt like a punch to his gut. If he had just taken Robert out on the highway when he'd had the chance, he wouldn't have been putting her back in another compromising position.

He should have killed him. He should have neutralized his pickup at the very least, but in that moment all he could think about was Holly and the situation she was in. He hated putting her in danger; and yet, here he was again, sifting through an impossible set of choices and trying to find the right answers to questions he never knew he'd be forced to face.

He unbuttoned his uniform shirt and slipped it off his shoulders.

"What are you doing?" she asked.

"Getting naked." He smirked. "Is that a problem?" he teased.

Her eyes widened and she opened her mouth to speak, but nothing came out.

"I'm kidding." He pulled his bulletproof vest off and handed it over to her. "You need to put this on."

She took his Kevlar vest and slipped it on over her head.

His body was warm where the vest had rested against his skin, and it brought him a certain amount of comfort to know that his warmth was against her. Even if it couldn't be his body, at least he was close to her.

He opened her door and helped her to pull the straps tight. "It's a little big, but I'd rather you have it on in case something happens."

She glanced up at him. "He's not in there, is he?"

He shook his head. "I don't think so, but I'm not gonna put you at risk. You keep that vest on until I tell you to take it off."

Or I take it off for you. Though it wasn't the most appropriate moment, his thoughts turned to him undressing her in the dark. If only things were different.

"Is it okay that I go in there? You know, with everything going on?" she asked, nibbling at her lip.

"I don't want you waiting out here alone. Just don't touch anything and please stick close to me."

The way he spoke made fear rise within her. "You don't really think that he's going to show up or anything, do you?"

It was definitely a possibility, especially if he had some kind of tech in his house that notified him upon their entry. Weasels had a way of popping up their heads when their territory was disturbed.

"I doubt it," he lied. "This is just to make me feel better."

She smiled at him, mollified.

He held out his hand and motioned for her to step out of the vehicle. Though he was aware that the other detective was likely watching them, he helped her slip from her seat before letting go of her hand.

He closed her door and grabbed his gear from the back seat. He pulled out his spare bulletproof vest and put it on, then put on his shirt and quickly buttoned it before slipping his bag over his shoulder.

Stowe walked over to them. "Holly this is Detective Josh Stowe, with DCI. Stowe, Holly."

Stowe gave her a tip of the head but didn't offer his hand.

"Let's roll." Ty motioned for the detective to follow them as they crossed the street and moved toward the door. He knocked, announcing their presence. There was no sound coming from inside. He reached down and unholstered his weapon. "Holly," he said, turning to face her. "You stay right there. We have to clear the structure. Okay?"

She nodded in understanding.

"Stowe, you ready?" he asked the detective.

The man tipped his head. "Let's do this." He stepped around Holly, giving her a gentle reassuring smile that made Ty like the guy a little more. He might have been a bit too big for his britches, but at least he was still a good human.

He went to the door and tried the knob. It was unlocked—at least he didn't have to kick it in. He opened the door a crack. "Robert Finch, this is the Madison County Sheriff's Department, we are here with a warrant to search your residence. If you are present, come out with your hands in the air!" he ordered.

Holly sucked in a breath behind him as he reached down and opened the unlocked front door. The finding surprised him. It wasn't entirely unusual for people not to lock their doors in Montana, but it was unusual for a suspect in an attempted homicide.

The smell hit him first. It was unmistakable. The coppery-metallic odor filled his senses and settled as a faint taste on his tongue. *Blood. Lots of blood.*

He glanced back over his shoulder at Stowe as he entered the house, looking to see if the other man sensed it, as well.

"Holy—" Stowe muttered. "Are you getting that, too?"

He nodded, looking into the entryway. To his left was a living room, which led to the main area of the house. In front of him was a typical entrance, a coatrack and a closet then at the far end of the little hallway was a set of stairs. At the top step, dripping down the beige carpet was a long trail of red. From their angle it was hard to say with any certainty, but if he had to guess the blood's source was probably lying just out of sight at the top.

He considered stopping and calling in more units, but there weren't any to spare. They had to handle this.

"Robert Finch, if you are inside the residence, put your hands up and step out where we can see you!" he ordered, louder than before in some hope that the source of the blood wasn't the man who'd gone missing.

There was no answer, not even the barking of a dog in the neighbor's yard. It was eerily quiet, so quiet that he could hear his own breathing and the racing of his heart.

He wasn't known for being nervous in these kinds of situations. If anything, he was typically cool under pressure, but Holly was throwing everything out of whack— she shouldn't have been there. He glanced behind him at her, but she was standing to the side of the open door and all he could see was the back of her hand and part of her side. It appeared as though she had her back turned to them and was peering out into the street.

He motioned for Stowe to close the door. She didn't need to witness what they were walking into. At least he could protect her from that.

He gestured toward the stairs as Stowe closed the door and kept it open just a crack. He liked the guy's style.

They cleared the living room to their left, then the kitchen and the rest of the ground floor of the house. Everything except the blood stain seemed normal and mostly well-kept. Nothing on the main floor gave him the impression that there had been any sort of struggle or fight.

His ankle cracked as he started to ascend the stairs. Nearing the top, he called out to Robert again, hoping the man would reply or appear in the event he was still alive or in the house. Again, he was met with eerie silence.

At first glance, he could make out a trail of the crimson liquid trickling down the hall and disappearing into the furthest bedroom on the left.

A giant black blow fly buzzed toward him, landing on his shoulder.

He hated flies.

Flies only meant one thing—they were nearing a death scene.

Clearing the hall and the other bedrooms, they worked toward what was a possible crime scene. As they neared the bedroom door, the drone of flies grew louder. He cringed at the sound; it was the same sound that frequented his nightmares. There was the faint aroma of decay, the kind that came with a recent death. For that, he was grateful. If they were finding death it was far better to find it sooner rather than later.

The bedroom door was closed, and he tapped on it, hoping against hope that he would get an answer. Instead, he only heard the buzzing of flies.

He reached down and touched the cold metal handle. Turning it, the door drifted open. The flies lifted into the air in a little black cloud of wings and bodies. There, on the floor in the master bedroom, next to the bed was Robert's dead body. Under his jaw was a small, tattooed edge gunshot wound. Blood was coming out of his mouth and stained the front of his white shirt and jeans. The injury was deadly, but it mustn't have killed him instantly as he may have walked from where they had initially encountered the blood trail—or, someone had moved him.

At the edge of the hole, a black fly moved. Ty waved his hand, shooing it off.

Near Robert's right hand was a Glock 19.

If he had to make a split-second judgment, it appeared as though Robert had committed suicide. However, after years working in law enforcement, he'd learned that the causes of deaths weren't always as they appeared.

Chapter Thirteen

She couldn't believe Robert was dead. In all the ways she imagined things unfolding with the man who'd fired at them earlier in the day, finding him shot in his bedroom wasn't even near the top of her list of likelihoods. Robert had always seemed like the kind of guy who loved himself too much to commit suicide.

Then again, Ty had made it clear that until they were done with their investigation, it wouldn't be known with certainty whether or not he had pulled the trigger or if someone else had.

She stood outside the house, looking at the open black body bag and Robert's remains. Due to the state of rigor, they hadn't been able to zip the bag all the way. Ty had placed paper bags around the dead man's hands, explaining it had been done to keep any evidence on his hands from being contaminated or altered while the body was in transit.

Robert's eyes were closed and aside from the blood and the hole, he could have just been asleep.

Ty touched her arm, drawing her attention. "Why don't you come with me?" he asked. "Stowe is going to take this. We can get out of here and you can get some rest."

She didn't want to rest. She didn't want to leave. If

anything, she wanted to make absolutely sure the man who had wanted her dead was placed in that body bag.

Robert had been a friend; they'd spent late nights in the office working out details and treatment plans and now she found herself questioning it all.

He had wanted to sleep with her, that much she had always known. However, she had also assumed he had put his feelings aside when she'd refused his advances.

Everything he'd ever done was for sex.

She was such a fool.

He was—wait, *had been*—such a creep. And somehow she had fallen for a number of his charms and allowed herself to become a victim and luckily a survivor of a failed murder attempt.

She could never trust anyone again.

It struck her how it was the people she knew best who had always proven to be the most dangerous.

At the thought, she glanced over at Ty. Maybe he was different. He cared about her. He was selfless. Maybe those perceived qualities were what made him just as gullible as her.

The coroner went to Robert's shoulders and started to move the body. The dead man let out a sigh. The sound made her jump.

Though she had known bodies did strange things after death, she hadn't heard that sound before.

Ty sighed. "Let's get out of here."

She nodded, satisfied that the man was really gone, and she wouldn't have to see him again.

Ty took her hand and led her down the stairs and out of the house, leaving Stowe and the coroner behind. She took one last look at Robert's house after she got in the truck, and they started to head down the road.

It struck her how strange her life had become. In just a matter of days, everything had come undone and her boring, normal life had turned into something she could have never imagined.

She should have never gone skiing.

Ty reached over and took her hand. "Do you want to go back to your place?"

She nodded, as the thought of all that she had experienced and felt for the last day moved through her. She was suddenly completely and utterly exhausted.

Her gaze fluttered down to Ty's hand. Something good had come from this, even if it was something she couldn't really explore. She gripped him tighter, as if that simple action would keep him in her life even though they both had to know how futile an attempt at a relationship would be between them.

It didn't take long before they were pulling into her driveway, and he was shifting into Park. She yawned, covering it with her free hand as she looked out at the dark windows of her place.

He strode around to her side and helped her out of the truck. It was such a little thing, but he'd done it earlier as well and it warmed her heart. He really was a great man. She loved that he was a gentleman and that he honestly seemed to care about what he did, the cases he was involved in and her.

As they walked toward her house and the moment they would have to say good-night, she couldn't remember exactly why they hadn't worked out before. It was all just some cloudy memory of the past, hazy and muted by time and experience.

She stepped to her front door, unsure of what to say or how to end their time together. There was always the option of inviting him in, as well. Her thoughts went to his kiss and the way she had opened to him. If she let him in, things between them would move to the bedroom. As much as she wanted him and to re-create that kiss, she wasn't sure she was in the right emotional space to make such a rash decision.

He moved beside her and took the keys from her as she went to unlock the door. "I've got it for you." He smiled at her, but there was a question in his eyes that made her wonder if he was having the same jumble of thoughts and feelings she was. He was probably questioning whether or not he even wanted to spend another second in her life.

He unlocked the door and looked back at her. "I know this is probably unnecessary, but do you mind if I clear your house before I go? I just want to reassure myself, more than anything."

"Robert..."

"Is dead. Yes. I know." He nodded. "I just can't ignore the knot in my gut."

She'd not been nervous about her safety in coming home. No, she'd been nervous about other things involved in Ty's being here, but now that he'd brought up questions around her coming back, she found she was nervous about them, as well.

"You don't think Robert like *booby-trapped* my house or anything, do you?" She frowned.

He smiled; the action was forced but somehow still reassuring. "I don't think he was that smart or had any of this planned out. When we get the toxicology reports from his autopsy, I bet that we will learn that he had some sort of chemicals rolling through his system."

"You think he was on drugs?"

"Drugs or a mental breakdown—either way..." His voice tapered off.

Either way, Robert was dead.

What he was saying made sense, but it went against his need to clear her house. If he didn't think that Robert had acted in a premeditated manner, then why did he feel the need to make sure she was still safe? She wanted to ask, but at the same time, she found a sense of relief in his wanting to stick around.

It was nice not being alone after a day like this.

She stepped in through her open front door and made her way inside. Her cat, Chubs, a gray tabby with a belly so round that it slung pendulum-like, strode toward them. He meowed loudly, protesting how much she'd been absent lately.

"That's Chubs," she said, motioning to her cat. "He likes people, but he drools when he is happy so watch out."

Ty came inside and closed the door. He walked over toward the cat and started scratching behind the little guy's ears. The sight tugged at Holly's heartstrings. There was just something about watching the sexy brunette man bending down, his jeans stretched tight over his ass as he cupped her cat's little fuzzy face in his hand. Chubs leaned into his hand and a little bead of drool started to slip from the corner of his mouth.

She laughed. "I warned you. And now that he knows you're a soft touch, good luck having an empty lap. He is a cuddler."

Ty stood up and brushed the loose cat hair off his hands. "I don't mind a lap full of kitty."

There was a lilt to his statement that made heat rise in her cheeks. She wasn't sure that he had meant it to sound dirty, but her sometimes unevolved brain went to the lowest hanging fruit.

"He may not be the only kitty in your lap, if you play your cards right," she teased, unable to help herself as she giggled.

Now, he was the one with a flush in his cheeks.

Two could play his torrid game.

"I…*er*… I won't be long," he said, turning his back as he reached up and lowered the zipper of his jacket.

She smiled, loving the fact that she had gotten to him. "You can take all the time you need."

Her house had been built in the 1970s and it was an open floor plan. The primary bedroom was isolated in the far corner of the house with a large walk-in closet and a huge en suite bathroom complete with a jetted tub and a glass-enclosed shower and an electric fireplace. Her bedroom and bathroom areas were her oasis. There was no better feeling than coming home after a long day at the office and sinking into a large bubble bath.

On really hard days, she would even have a chilled glass of chardonnay while she tried to soak the stressors of the day away.

Ty had his hand on the gun at his waist, and the way he roll stepped through her house made her think about him clearing Robert's house only hours before.

How long would it take before things would get back to normal and everything wouldn't remind her of the trauma of this day?

Probably never.

Time could heal a lot of things, but she doubted it would clear her of the memories of a murder attempt and a dead potential killer.

From the time they'd been shot at to the time he'd been

found dead in his house, he could have only been down for maybe an hour.

It was strange now that she thought about it. Heck, it was cold outside. Where did the flies even come from?

Ty made his way over to the two guest bedrooms, opening the doors and peering inside. They didn't have much, a bed on the carpet and each had cheap dressers she'd picked up at IKEA the last time she'd made her way through Seattle on the way to Portland to see her college friends. That must have been at least five years ago.

"You have a really nice home."

"Thanks," she said. "I'm lucky my parents left the place to me—if they hadn't, it would have been tough to buy. Everything has gotten so expensive thanks to the great migration to the western states."

"Yeah," he said, nodding. "You are lucky."

"I always wanted to come back to Big Sky and when I got the opportunity to be a partner at Spanish Peaks Physical Therapy, I was grateful to have a place waiting."

"Was Robert working there when you started?" he asked, walking toward her bedroom.

"He took his position two years after I bought into the practice." She walked to the kitchen, trying to control her anxiety from creeping up into her core thanks to him getting so close to her bedroom. She could only imagine how she would feel if she was leading the way through that door.

His hand tightened on the grip of his gun, his finger twitching over the release on his holster as he moved through her bedroom door and into her private oasis.

"Have you notified the staff about Robert's death?" he asked.

She shook her head. "I've been getting texts from Stephanie. It sounds like word has already reached them."

He nodded, but his face was pinched. He stepped into her room and disappeared.

She thought about the teddy bear that sat in the center of her pillows on her bed. *Oh, for the love of all that was good in this world, don't let him see the damned bear.*

It had been a gift from her late father, but she didn't want to answer questions as to why a grown woman still had a stuffed animal on her bed. It was juvenile and as far from sexy as she could possibly be.

If she'd been thinking maybe she could have side-tracked Ty long enough to pitch the furry thing under the bed before he'd cleared her room. Then again, he was *clearing* her room. There was no way that he would have let her go inside the room without him stopping her.

She heard the click of her bathroom door opening and the thud of his footfalls on her marble floor. *That bathroom.* She sighed.

He moved around the bathroom and then there was a long moment before he made his way back out to the living room, and her. His hand was off his gun like his search had revealed nothing—and the simple act was enough to make her relax.

He was almost as good as a hot bath.

She smiled thinking about their kiss in his truck. "Anything?" she asked, though she already knew the answer.

Don't say anything about the teddy bear... Don't say anything... She repeated in her mind.

He walked over toward her and stopped, putting his hand on her lower back. The action was so unexpected and so sexy that she felt her knees actually grow weak. Until now, she wasn't sure that she had even believed such a thing was real—especially when it was caused by a mere touch.

She turned around, letting his hand slip around to the front of her belly. It made her breath catch. His gaze was on his hand and where her T-shirt had risen and exposed a thin strip of her naked skin. His eyes moved up, and he stared into hers.

She'd forgotten she was wearing her coat until this moment. Inside it, she felt like she was boiling. A bead of sweat slipped down from the base of her hair and down her neck.

"I…I'm *hot*." She stepped back, away from his touch and the effect it was having on her.

She pulled off her jacket and placed it on the coatrack by the back door, which led out of the kitchen and toward her detached garage.

Glancing out toward the garage, she spotted a light shining out of the side window and reflecting off the snow. She didn't remember leaving the light on out there. In fact, if she had, it would have been on all day. It was totally possible that when she'd gone out there this morning, she'd flicked on the lights and forgotten them. It wouldn't have been the first time thanks to the dark winter days in Montana.

She motioned toward the light. "I…I need to go outside."

He looked out the window and in the direction she pointed. "Oh, I can get it for you." He smiled, but he opened and closed the hand which had just been grazing her skin. "If you want, we can have a warm drink together when I come back inside. Coffee?"

She glanced at the top of her refrigerator where a bottle of whiskey sat, dusty from the last time she'd even been tempted to have a finger. "If you want, I can make us hot toddies."

"Whiskey?" His grin widened. "You must be ready to call it a night."

"I think I earned a stiff one." The heat moved up from her core again, but she embraced her embarrassment. She wanted him to be as uncomfortable with their proximity and this night as she was.

He laughed, the sound throaty and rough. "I got it for you."

He did not just say that.

He motioned toward the garage. "I mean the light... I've got the light."

She stared at him and the redness in his cheeks.

"I'm sure you do." She took a step toward him, but he rushed toward the back door, pulling up the zipper on his jacket.

As the door clicked shut behind him and he rushed out into the darkness toward the garage, she couldn't help but feel like once again she'd made another mistake. This time, she'd come on too strong.

TY CLICKED OFF the light in her detached garage and let the cold, wintery night air wash over his fevered skin. Holly wanted him. There was no doubt that if he walked back in that house that they would end up in bed together. A bed complete with a stuffed animal.

He smiled as he thought of the bear. Then there was Chubs the cat. He barely knew that damned creature and he already loved it.

If he went back in that house, not only would he be opening his heart to Holly, but he would be opening his heart to her entire world and all the chaos that came with it. But how could he judge her for her life when his was far busier and all-over-the-map than hers.

No two days at his job were the same. He never really left the office on time. His last relationship had crashed and burned because of his deep commitment to the sheriff's department. There was always some case, some family, some investigation that required his attention. He was pulled in so many directions.

She needed a man who would come home for dinner every night, a man who knew when he would need to work, and one who had weekends off to take her on dates. She needed a man who could hold her in his arms as they drifted off to sleep.

He would never be that man. He was married to his job.

He looked back at the house. Thanks to the darkness in her backyard, he could stare straight into her kitchen window. She was standing at the kitchen island, probably making them drinks.

Drinks.

Oh, we will definitely end up in the sack.

He stood there, staring at that kitchen window for far too long.

In fact, it was so long that he started to get cold. He was in complete darkness and he watched her search the night for him. He didn't move. He didn't want to hurt her or let her down, but he also found himself not wanting her to see he was out there.

This thing between them, whatever it was, was precarious. He had an unspoken rule about never going back to exes, but he'd already stepped in front of that train the moment he'd kissed her.

As she turned away from the window, he could have

sworn that instead of concern, he saw a look of relief on her face. That was enough.

He knew what had to be done.

He slipped out of the backyard and toward his pickup. He started it up and rolled to the end of her road, just out of sight of her place. He stopped and pulled out his phone. He sent her a simple text. I'll see you in the morning.

He waited for a response, but he was met with silence.

Chapter Fourteen

Holly tried to tell herself that his disappearance in the night didn't bother her. That his leaving was the smartest thing either of them could have done. Moreover, she tried to convince herself that the ache in her chest and the pain that she felt at his rejection was just a figment of her imagination. She didn't care that he'd left her. Alone. Waiting. Wanting him.

Gah.

She hadn't slept well. And though she was aware it was petty, she hoped he hadn't slept well, either. At the very least, she hoped that he stared at the ceiling for a while, second-guessing his choice.

She highly doubted it, though.

He was always the guy who had his act together. Always so damned perfect.

She'd never measure up to him. She'd always be the lesser if they ever thought about dating again.

Yet, if he was so *perfect* then why had he kissed her? A perfect man wouldn't have done what he'd done and then left her waiting in her kitchen for him to come back from the garage. If anything, he was a coward.

She could do better than a coward.

However, a coward wouldn't have interceded the other night with Robert on her doorstep.

Robert.

His body was now resting in a cooler somewhere and here she was worried about some ridiculous kiss.

Yes, that's what it was…*ridiculous.* And she was ridiculous for thinking it was anything more than some impulsive decision. Ty'd probably not even given it another thought. If anything, he was probably the kind of guy who kissed a woman whenever the opportunity arose. Opportunities she was sure came quite often. He was far too charming and entirely too handsome for women not to fall upon his feet…*or onto somewhere else for that matter.*

The thought of his assumed bedroom activities made a spike of jealousy pierce through her. How dare he be with all these other women?

Especially when she wanted him.

Err…

No, she didn't want him. And none of this mattered.

She slammed her coffee cup down too hard on the counter and it splashed up, all over her face. Hot coffee dripped down her cheek. A droplet had even landed on her eyelashes.

"Damn it…" she cussed, irritated with herself and her feelings and thoughts.

She was never skiing again.

But…she loved to ski.

She wiped up the coffee on her marble countertop. There was a tap on the door, the sound making her jump.

If that was Ty, she was going to give him a piece of her mind. She huffed as she flipped the kitchen towel over her shoulder and stomped toward the door.

Standing on the other side of the door was Detective Stowe.

"Detective," she said in greeting, slightly taken aback by his sudden presence in her doorway. "How can I help you?" She opened the door wide and stepped out of the way and motioned for him to come inside.

"Hello, Ms. Dean, how are you doing this morning?" he asked, stepping inside from the cold as she shut the door behind him.

"I'm fine. Surprised to see you. Is everything okay?" She paused as a horrible thought struck her and made her stomach sour. "Is *Ty* okay?"

He nodded, waving her off. "Absolutely, he's just fine. In fact, I don't even think he knows I'm here this morning. I haven't spoken to him since the last time I saw you two."

A sense of relief washed over her. So many things had gone wrong in her life, and she could have dealt with any number more, but Ty getting hurt would definitely push her over the edge.

"Would you like some coffee?" she asked. "I was just having some," she said, pointing toward the kitchen.

The detective smiled. "I can see that," he said, motioning toward her shirt and the coffee stain on her breast. "And thanks for the offer, but I already had my cup for the day."

She dabbed at the coffee with the towel on her shoulder. "*Gah.* I'm such a mess lately."

The man motioned to sit on her sofa. She gave him a nod and sat across from him in her large leather chair. She leaned on the armrest and pulled her feet up and beside her.

"So, if you didn't come here for my coffee, how can I help you?"

He scratched at the back of his neck; the action almost seemed like a nervous tic rather than a real itch for him to scratch. "By chance did either you or Ty see Robert driving yesterday?"

She looked up and to the left as she tried to recall everything that had happened when they'd been shot at. "I never saw his face, but I did see the driver once. He was wearing sunglasses and a hat."

The detective nodded. "Interesting. Can you say that you were absolutely sure it was Robert you saw in his pickup?"

She frowned. "I saw, wait *we both* saw who we believed to be Robert. Why?"

"Okay, but you never saw his face?"

She shook her head and suddenly found herself questioning everything about what had happened. She'd once watched a *Nova* science show about memory and how every time someone recalled a memory it was reformed in the psyche. When it happened, glitches occurred and mistakes were made, often in line with what a person *wished* had happened. It was an interesting science, but she had no idea how quickly it would change her memory. It had only been a day, but then how did perspective come into play?

What it all boiled down to was the fact that she couldn't say with utmost certainty that she *had* actually seen Robert. What she had seen was Robert's truck, and someone driving it.

"If it wasn't Robert, who do you think was driving the truck? Who shot at us?"

The detective shrugged, but he couldn't meet her gaze. It made her wonder if he had an idea, but just couldn't tell her. "You know the interesting part of all of this is that I

ran a check on Robert and didn't find any weapons registered to him. I have a guy running a ballistics analysis
on the slugs we managed to pull out of the little coffee
shop and from the body of Ty's pickup. It will be interesting to see what he comes back with."

She nodded, but all she wanted to do right now was
talk to Ty so he could help her make sense of all of this.
So, he could corroborate what they had seen.

"I think you need to talk to Ty." She paused, picking
at a string on the cuff of her shirt. "May I ask why you
came to me with these questions first? It surprises me."

The detective smiled, as though she had caught him
in some kind of maneuver. "I can definitely see why Ty
likes you. You're clever."

That didn't really answer her question. "And?"

She didn't mean to come off sharp or snarling with
the detective, but she couldn't help it. She didn't like the
feeling of platitudes and inauthenticity. She also didn't
like the thought of the detective taking note of whatever
was happening between her and Ty. What happened between them or didn't happen wasn't the man's business.
Then again, he was a detective, and he was the one inves-
tigating the shooting as well as Robert's death. Perhaps
their relationship had a direct impact on his investigation.

The thought made her stomach ache.

She could only imagine standing in front of a judge
explaining what was or wasn't happening between her
and Ty. She had known she was playing with fire, and
she had still managed to find herself in this position. If
only she had listened to her intuition and had not gotten involved physically. When she saw him again, she'd
have to explain all the reasons they couldn't be together.

"I just wanted to hear things from your perspective before I reached out to Ty. I wanted…" He paused.

"What you wanted was to find deviations between his story and mine. I don't know what you think is going on, or what we did or didn't do, but we have done nothing wrong."

He put his hands up. "Whoa. I don't think that either of you had any direct role in Robert's death. I don't want you to think that for a second."

She had liked Detective Stowe, but he was making her upset. Or maybe, it wasn't he who was upsetting her, rather it was the entire situation.

There was a knock at the door. "That's probably him."

The detective nodded, then dipped his chin in the direction of the sound of the knock like she was free to answer. She tried not to be annoyed as she got up and opened her front door. Ty was standing there with his back turned to her, as he stared out at Stowe's rig.

He turned and gave her a guilty smile.

She was suddenly all too aware that he'd left her waiting last night, but now wasn't the time for them to talk about it. She pointed at the detective's Tahoe. "Obviously, your buddy is here." She motioned for Ty to come inside and close the door behind him.

Stowe stood up and extended his hand to Ty as he walked into the living room. "Hey, Ty, how's it going this morning?" Detective Stowe asked as they shook hands.

"Good, but I could ask you the same question." Ty frowned.

Ty instinctively stepped in front of Holly like he could shield her from harm. She had been right in being concerned that the detective had come here before speaking to him first.

"I was going to give you a call as soon as I left."

Ty crossed his arms over his chest and the simple action made him appear bigger than he had two seconds before. His pecs were pressed against his shirt, and she found herself wanting to touch them to see if they were as muscular and hard as they looked.

Not now. She shook off the thought.

"I'm sure I was on your mind."

He is certainly on mine. Her mouth had watered so much that she was forced to swallow. *I'm being ridiculous.*

She felt warmth move up into her face as Ty looked over at her and winked. He must have noticed her staring.

Detective Stowe stepped away from the couch. "I was going to call and tell you about Robert's remains and the initial assessment we got back from the medical examiner." He pointed toward the kitchen. "Do you want to talk with me, privately?"

"Just talk, unless you think one of us had something to do with it." He lifted a brow in a challenge.

Stowe sniffed. "No. I don't have reason to believe anything of the sort. So far, it does look like his death was a suicide. However, the time of death has left me with a great deal of questions."

"Okay?" Ty countered. "Why?"

"Well, according to the ME, Robert died in the early hours of the morning."

The strangeness of the time of his death wasn't lost on her. He had killed himself not long after they'd fought on her doorstep.

If Detective Stowe learned about their altercation, would it change his mind about Robert's death being a suicide?

If she told him about what had transpired, she would

quickly become his number one murder suspect. She looked to Ty who gently nodded, like he was also thinking about what had happened with Robert on her doorstep.

He leaned closer so only she could hear him as he whispered. "Tell him."

She took in a gulp of air, feeling that in some ways it could be her last as a free woman. "Detective Stowe?" she started, sounding meeker than she would have liked.

"Yes. What is it?" he asked, tenting his fingers as he looked intently at her.

"Robert came over here…the night that I was found on the mountain. We had a fight."

His eyebrows rose, but his expression was neutral. His gaze remained on her face. "Do you mind telling me what the fight was about?"

She glanced over at Ty. "He… I…"

"He was infatuated with her," Ty said, speaking for her.

Stowe looked over at him with a touch of condemnation on his face for Ty's interference. "Were you there?"

Ty cleared his throat uncomfortably. "I witnessed them on the front porch when I rolled by after the callout. I wanted to make sure she had made it home safely." He picked at the edge of his shirt cuff, but quickly stopped himself and held his hands together. "Robert was angry. He was hitting the doorjamb and yelling in her face. I knew that I needed to step in before the situation escalated."

Stowe nodded. He opened up his phone and took down a series of notes. Watching him made her gut ache.

He turned back to her. "What was Robert upset about?"

"He…" She hated that she had to say it all out loud. "He wanted to be with me. I kept saying no, but he wouldn't listen."

Stowe tapped on his screen and then looked between Holly and Ty. "I hope you two know that this makes things a bit more complicated—you may be the last people who saw Robert alive."

Chapter Fifteen

Ty watched from the window as Detective Stowe pulled out of Holly's driveway and hit the road. He'd made sure the door hadn't hit the guy on the way out, but he hadn't been sad to see him leave.

He couldn't believe what the detective had told them. If Robert had been dead long before they'd been shot at, there was no way that he had been the one to pull the trigger. But who else would want them dead?

As an officer of the law there were certainly a number of people who didn't like him. However, he hadn't received any credible death threats and, while he was working on a variety of cases, most people seemed to understand he was just doing his job.

One of the mothers he'd recently worked with had come to pick up her son's belongings after he was found dead in the woods. She had been angry that they hadn't gotten to him when he was still alive, but he had taken the time and once again explained that their being in the woods had happened as rapidly as possible.

That case had been a tough one.

As it had turned out, the kid had decided to take his own life after a girl had broken his heart.

Understandably, his mom had been distraught and had

a tough time processing the circumstances that had contributed to her son's death.

He'd never forget when he'd initially told her what happened. She had hit her knees and yelled and screamed and damned him, but it had just been her agony talking.

"Holly...is there anyone from your life who would want to hurt you?" Ty asked.

She chewed at her lip. "Not that I can think of...but everything in my life has been turned upside down."

"And I know I've asked you before, but..."

Her entire body tensed.

"Was there any kind of relationship between you and Robert? The only reason I'm asking is that it is *highly* unusual for someone to act like he had when there'd been no previous *romantic* relationship."

She couldn't meet his gaze.

Her inability to look at him told him that he'd been right...there was something she had been hiding.

"Did you sleep with him?" he pressed, knowing he had hit on something, even if it was something he didn't really want to hear.

"I...I let him kiss me. It was a few months ago. Things went further than they should have. And, well..."

"He thought it was true love?"

She shrugged, but from the way her shoulders hunched, she agreed with his assessment.

"You should have told me before." He hated the fact that she had tried to conceal anything from him. Especially something like her relationship with Robert. It was critical to the investigation.

If she could lie about something so important, what else was she capable of lying about?

"I just didn't think it was that important."

"Were you talking to him all the time? Texting or whatever?" He had to push the issue. He had to know what else she wasn't telling him.

Her chin dropped lower to her chest. "We worked together. We were friends. I made it clear I wasn't interested in a romantic relationship."

"But you were talking to him daily?"

She nodded, not looking at him.

"Multiple times a day?"

She nodded again, her chin now resting on her chest in shame.

"Okay, got it." He huffed a sigh.

"I wasn't trying to string him along. I wasn't interested in him like that." Her voice quaked. She finally looked up at him as she spoke.

"But you knew he wanted something more and you continued to talk to him?"

She furrowed her brows. "What happened... It wasn't my fault. He was the one who wouldn't take no for an answer."

He stared straight into her eyes. "Never...not for one second...would I think that what has happened was *your fault*. I think Robert had some issues. Unfortunately, he targeted you."

She shook her head. "That's what I don't understand though... I know for a fact that he would go out with other women. He was a player."

"How do you know?"

Anger flickered over her features. "He would tell me about all these women who he'd gone out with."

"And it upset you?"

She huffed. "No. I saw it for what it was—some kind

of manipulation tactic to show me how desirable he was, and what I was missing out on."

"I can safely say that I don't think you were missing out on a thing with him." He tried not to let his anger slip into his voice, but he wasn't sure it was working. "Do you remember any of the women who he said he was seeing?"

"It would be easier to ask who he *wasn't* claiming to date in the town."

"But you don't think he was actually going on those dates, or do you?"

She grabbed her empty cup and moved to take it to the kitchen. "I think that he was willing to do anything in order to attempt to get under my skin."

"Or in your bed."

She nodded, as she sat the white porcelain cup on the top of the couch and looked at him. "I don't understand men." She ran her finger over the rim. "Did he really think that his being with other women would make me want to run into his arms?"

"I think he just wanted your attention—negative attention is better than none at all." He thought about the last run-in he'd had with Robert when he'd been at this house. "I mean, just look at his display on your front porch. He *had* to have known that wasn't going to advance your relationship, but that didn't stop him from making a scene."

She tapped the cup with her fingers, making a hollow sound. "It also didn't stop him from taking his own life." She glanced over at him, and he could see the pain in her eyes. "Why is death following me?"

"It's not following you; we are both at its epicenter."

She nodded. "Have you ever heard that these things always happen in threes?"

He'd heard the old wives' tale, but he didn't know how

much he believed the adage—death was a constant in his world. At this point the body count in his life was more in the hundreds than the single digits. "I have, but I don't put a lot of stock in it."

"I hope there's nothing to it." She picked up the cup and walked to the kitchen. "I don't want one of us to be next," she said the last line so quietly he was sure he wasn't supposed to hear.

He sure as hell wasn't going to let something like that happen.

As she disappeared into the kitchen, he pulled out his phone and texted Stowe.

Do you have a list of the last numbers Robert had called? I'd like to look into the women in his life.

Stowe texted back almost instantly. working on it. Will get u the list as soon as judge signs off.

Holly came walking out of the kitchen, there was a towel still draped over her shoulder and he wondered for a moment if she had completely forgotten about it.

"I was thinking…what did the medical examiner say about Moose's lacerations? You kind of said something about it with Detective Stowe."

Ty nodded, but his stomach clenched as he thought about how their meeting had ended—and how their necks were close to the chopping block. "The ME emailed me the report this morning."

It struck him as odd that Holly would call Moose's cause of death lacerations; it sounded more like something he would have said. However, she'd been around him so much that he wondered if she was starting to pick up on his mannerisms.

In relationships and courtships, one of the common indicators that people had been together a long time, or they were very interested in one another, was that they mirrored each other. In effect, they would adopt mannerisms and gesticulations of their mate or desired mate, in order to create the bond.

Holly was likely doing this unintentionally, but whether it was intentional or not, he liked it. However, they were already bonded. They'd been bonded ever since they were young, foolish and flirting with the idea of dating like mature adults. It was just recently that their bond had truly intensified and moved past the puppy love they'd once shared.

He watched as she swept her blond hair back and away from her face. As she turned her neck, all he could think about was how he wanted to kiss the small hollow by the base of her ear. He could trail his lips down…

She didn't need to do anything else to make him want her more. As screwed up and as complicated as it was, he wanted her for everything that she embodied.

His mind went to what she had revealed about Robert.

It really wasn't her fault that a man had taken an interest in her—and an unsafe one, at that. He wasn't even upset that Robert had made a move—though the thought made him slightly nauseated. What he was upset with was her failure to be candid.

He should not have judged her for the kiss or the texting, but he *did*. He knew it wasn't okay, but it was hard not to feel like she had played a role in leading Robert on by continually texting.

If he'd been in her shoes, what would he have done?

They *were* coworkers. And based on what he did know about Robert, the dude had probably drawn her in—likely talking about something at work and then subtly testing his boundaries by flirting. He'd likely grown bolder until he was inappropriate, and she'd been forced to say something.

If that was the case, he could understand. And he could also understand why she wouldn't have wanted to admit what had happened—Robert had groomed her.

For now, the best thing he could do was get over his feelings of betrayal. This really wasn't her doing and she needed him to help her understand that and to help her work through her feelings.

"What else did they say?" she asked, pulling him from his turbulent thoughts.

"Who?"

"The medical examiner. About Moose?" she asked, sounding concerned by his lack of focus.

"Oh." He lifted his phone like she could read the email through the black screen. "They sent a little bit more information about the knife wound. It appears that the blade itself was about eight inches long and consistent with what would be a butcher knife shape."

Holly frowned. "A butcher knife? They're really big."

"I know, it's weird. Why would someone have a butcher knife on a mountainside?" He clicked on his phone and opened up the autopsy report, more so that he could control his feelings and thoughts of Holly and to concentrate on something he could better understand.

Holly walked over and sat on the couch, so close to him in the chair that their knees actually touched.

He didn't know if she was touching him on purpose, but regardless, he liked it.

"Did they find any other clues as to who would have

killed your friend?" she asked, leaning down and putting her elbows on her knees.

As she leaned forward, he could see down her blue V-neck shirt. The tops of her breasts were right there. So close... His mouth watered.

Clearing his throat, he stood up. He couldn't look at her like that. All willpower would be lost, and he had a job to do. Plus, she had lied to him.

He tried to remind himself of that as he turned around and realized he could see even farther down her shirt from his new vantage. "I'm going to go grab a glass of water. Do you need anything?"

She shook her head. As she moved, so did her breasts. Damn those breasts.

"I just can't stop thinking about that knife," she said as he walked away from her.

He wished he was thinking about a knife right now and not the places his mouth could be exploring.

"Oh?" he said, stepping into the kitchen and leaning against the wall while he tried to regain his composure.

"It's a strange knife and not very functional in the woods."

"Yeah, I agree." He straightened his shirt, pressing out invisible wrinkles. "Most of the people in my SAR unit only carry small fixed-blade knives or folding knives that are around a blade size of three inches or so. A butcher knife would be hard to carry, hard to conceal and hard to use in the event of taking down an animal or butchering. Something like that is more of a statement piece or something someone would use in more temperate climates for bushwhacking."

"Do you think that someone was just trying to scare Moose and things got out of control?" she called from the living room.

He grabbed a glass out of the cupboard and poured himself some water. He chugged it down like it could extinguish the flames of lust that coursed through him. Chubs bumped against his leg and he gave the cat a little scratch behind the ear.

"I have a hard time believing that Moose was murdered. I mean, I know he was, I just..." He sat the glass down and stared at the ripples on the surface of the remaining liquid. "He didn't have any enemies. He wasn't in a location where anyone could have gotten to him easily. And now this knife? Nothing about his death makes sense."

As he spoke, he gave Chubs one last scratch and stood up. Near the stove was a large knife block. One of knives was gone.

He opened the dishwasher and placed his glass on the top rack. The machine was empty, as was the sink—except for his glass and her cup.

Odd.

He closed the machine and glanced around the kitchen. The knife was nowhere to be seen. As he neared the black plastic block, he could read the name of the one that was missing—*Butcher Knife.*

He had a sinking feeling that the woman who had him seeking refuge in the kitchen, the woman he'd rescued and protected, could very well be the person who was responsible for his best friend's murder.

Chapter Sixteen

Ty was acting strange. Ever since they had talked to the detective, Ty had been off. One minute he was touching her and smiling and the next he was physically as far away from her as he could be without going outside, and he wouldn't meet her gaze.

She wanted to ask him what was wrong, but she already knew the answer—she had kept the truth of her and Robert's past a secret. It would be false to think she hadn't omitted details on purpose. She had certainly not intended on telling him everything—she had been afraid that if she told him everything, he would turn away from her and think that she had more with Robert than what had been there.

By not telling him, it had compounded the effects of her fears and made everything a thousand times worse. She should have told him the truth from the very beginning. If he hadn't liked her, or if he had judged her for the mistakes in her past, then he wasn't the man who was supposed to come into her life and remain. She just hadn't trusted that he would see past her faults.

Now, her faults were all he could see.

At one point, she had assumed that when she became an adult, life would get easier and *simpler*. Unfortunately, here she was trying to find love with the right man while also trying to escape the ravaging effects of love inflicted upon her by the wrong one.

She thought she'd handled things well, that she had done what was best to keep anyone from getting hurt—and yet, everyone in her life had either ended up dead or figuratively bloodied.

She didn't know what to do, or how to fix her mistakes. All she knew with any certainty was that she couldn't bring Robert or Moose back.

Maybe there was something about how Ty kept running away—not that he would call it that. However, when things got tough or they were growing closer, he had a way of just *disappearing*.

It seemed to have worked for him, maybe it would work for her, as well?

She glanced toward the kitchen and the back door that led out to the garage—the same place where Ty had disappeared when they'd been about to take things between them to the next physical level.

She'd forgiven him—heck, she'd even understood it. Why couldn't he come her way on this?

"Ty…" she started.

He twitched like she was striking him.

She hated the response and instantly wished she hadn't spoken his name.

"Yes?" he countered, but his feet were pointed directly at the front door like he was ready to run.

"I swear I was never interested in Robert and I'm sorry I didn't tell you everything from the beginning. I know you're mad, but I don't think it's okay for you to punish me."

He looked at her, his expression confused. "What?"

Is that not what he is upset with? she wondered, slightly taken aback.

She didn't want to repeat her statement if he didn't know what she was talking about. She didn't want to compound whatever problem they were having by adding more weight.

"You're obviously upset. What did I do?" she asked, earnestly.

His gaze flashed to the kitchen, but then he looked at her. He let out a long sigh. "I... Nothing. Don't worry about whatever happened between you and Robert—that guy was a real piece of work and I understand how you got in trouble with him." He walked toward the door.

She didn't know what he was doing, or where he was going, but it looked like he was once again running away. This time she wouldn't let him. Grabbing her coat, she followed in step behind him.

"What are you doing?" he asked, opening the door and moving to walk outside.

"I'm going with you. We started this investigation together, we are going to finish it together." She stood tall in her resolve. "After we are done, if you don't want to talk to me ever again then that's up to you."

He looked out at his pickup and then back at her. "Fine. Whatever."

THERE WERE ANY number of reasons that the butcher knife would have been missing from the knife block in Holly's kitchen. Ty wasn't entirely unreasonable. Yet, he couldn't stop thinking about the knife and what it *could have* meant. He thought about asking her about it and its absence, but he didn't want her to think that he was looking at her as a potential suspect or that she was complicit with the murder in any way—she was already struggling.

Holly wasn't a killer. She hadn't called in her own disappearance, and nothing pointed at her being involved in Moose's death—other than being the reason Moose had been on the mountain.

He had to be realistic, even if he was still freaked out.

His intuition told him something was very wrong and that the missing knife meant something. However, everything was just coincidental at this point. Everyone had those types of knives in their home, or at least most people did, and it's very possible that it had just been simply mislaid or put away in a drawer and he hadn't seen it. But there was just something in his gut that told him he needed to look deeper.

Then again, from the very moment he had brought Holly back into his life he'd been looking for reasons not to fall for her again. He'd been keeping her at arm's length, and now he was keeping her at blade length, as well.

As he drove toward the sheriff's department and his office, he made sure to keep his eyes on the road. He didn't want to give away his myriad of feelings and questions to Holly. It could hold. Maybe the knife would just show back up, too.

He pulled into his parking space in front of the department.

Holly hadn't said a word since they had gotten into the pickup. He appreciated it.

He got out and opened her door for her.

She looked at him with questions in her eyes, but he tried to ignore them. "Are you going to tell me why you're upset before we go inside? Or am I gonna have to play the guessing game until I figure it out for myself?" Holly asked.

He shut her door and locked his pickup. "I'll get over it. Don't worry about it."

Darkness took over her features. "I don't like this, Ty. I don't like not knowing what is going on inside you. At least give me a clue as to if I am in trouble with you or not. Is there something I can do to make things better between us? Did I say something?"

Her questions made him actually feel bad. Of course she would be questioning herself and all the things that she had done. To her, his coldness had to be strange.

"Seriously, I'll be fine. I just have a lot on my mind."

She frowned, clearly not believing him.

Before she could grill him further, he made his way to the doors leading to his office and went inside. She followed behind him in close step. As he used his badge to gain access to the authorized area, several of the office ladies took interest and stared in their direction. Of course, they would be curious. Since Holly had last been in here, the women of the office had probably learned exactly who she was, and thanks to the small-town gossip mill, they probably also knew about his and Holly's past relationship.

Nothing stayed a secret very long—especially when it came to the office drama.

He gave the ladies a small tip of the head in acknowledgment as he made his way back to his office and his waiting stack of papers.

They could think whatever they wanted. Holly was a blast from his past and now a possible suspect. If they wanted to think anything besides that, it was on them.

He closed his office door behind them and motioned for Holly to take a seat across from him at his desk. "I'm going to go over everyone who was on scene the day of

Moose's death. Most people work in and around here, but it may take a few hours to go through everyone."

She nodded in understanding. "What can I do to help?"

In truth, he wanted to see her reaction so he could tell if there was anything to the knot in his stomach.

"Listen… Maybe you can find something I'm missing." *Or, something you are*, he thought, but he quickly rebuked himself.

He pulled up the list of SAR members and the report his boss, Cindy, had written about their callout. All the names on the list were familiar and he knew all the people so well that it felt obtrusive and a touch like madness as he started with the first name on his list—Cindy herself.

As he moved to call her, he looked over at Holly. "I know it's a big ask, but would you run down the hall and grab me a drink?"

He was fine, but he needed a minute of privacy.

As though Holly saw right through his ask, she nodded. "I'll give you some time." She motioned to the hall. "I'll be right outside when you're done."

He wanted to tell her that she was wrong, but he couldn't lie. "Thanks," he said with a weak smile. "It won't take me long on the phone here."

She stood up and gave him a terse nod before stepping out of his office and closing the door.

Cindy answered her phone on the first ring. Probably recognizing his office number, she bypassed the niceties. "Did you figure out what happened to Moose?" she asked the second she came on the line.

He huffed. "I was hoping you had," he joked, trying to ease the tension between them and make light of what had happened as much as possible.

"I've been going through everything that happened out

there. It just doesn't make sense." There was the sound of cars, like Cindy was driving while she was on the phone.

"I hear you. It's a strange ordeal, the whole thing." He paused. "I read over your report of the callout. You did a nice job. Thorough. Detective Stowe is using it to help conduct his investigation into the death, as well."

"You aren't handling this in-house?" she asked.

"No, too many problems if we did." That was an understatement. If he conducted the investigation, it would be a conflict of interest. And, if this thing was never solved, then he would have to bear the weight of their not knowing what had actually happened to his friend for the rest of his life.

Moose's mother, Rebecca, would never forgive him.

"So, I did a little digging around, about our friend Moose. According to the people at the grange, Moose had been frequenting the bar with a few different women. One of them was none other than our Miss Valerie."

The news didn't surprise him. Valerie was a member of the SAR team, but she had made a point of always saying she was never interested in dating Moose. It wasn't a secret that most of the time she and Moose barely tolerated each other. But maybe that was why they had gone out drinking together, maybe they had some kind of love-hate relationship. He didn't think they were sleeping together but he hadn't talked to Valerie directly about it.

"I'll look into that. Thanks for the heads-up."

"Do you think that Stowe can handle this? Or are you gonna run with the ball?"

"Like I said, Stowe is running with it, but I've definitely been putting in some legwork. Unfortunately, I have another new case. With everything happening, we need all hands on deck."

"I get it. If you find that you need anything else from me don't hesitate." Cindy hung up the phone.

He really did like her. She was definitely a person with no fluff or falseness.

According to the department's schedule, Valerie should be in the office soon. So, he gave her a quick call, but it went straight to her cell phone's voice mail. He left a quick message asking her just to call him back.

Though it was an interesting lead, he really did have a tough time thinking that Valerie would have let Moose into her bed. Then again, proximity, availability and the number of drinks they both had could have overridden both of their better judgments. It was something he had seen before, and as he thought about Holly, he could understand a person acting against their better judgment.

If Valerie and Moose had been a thing, it still wouldn't explain his death. Valerie didn't seem like the jealous type, and if she had hurt Moose, he was surprised that she would have done it in such an ill-conceived manner. She worked in law enforcement as an evidence tech, if she had done something like commit homicide, she would have been clean about it.

He followed up his call to Valerie by calling the rest of the team. Everyone else was helpful and Smash had even reminded him that he could pull the GAIA, their team's GPS mapping system, that each of them had used to follow their movements while on their callout that night.

To garner the information, he didn't even need a subpoena. All he had to do was reach out to their mapping expert. It would be simple to clear everyone.

He felt like an idiot for not thinking about it earlier. Yet, it wasn't something he had dealt with before. Typically, on a mission, tracking was just a matter of policy in case something went to court. It wasn't until after the fact, and in the hands of armchair quarterbacks, that it was frequently used.

He decided to give himself grace on this one. He had been dealing with a lot of events, which led to even more directions. None of them simple.

He called their mapping expert who aggregated the data, Sharon Cleaver.

"Heya, Ty, how's it going?" she chirped.

She was in her forties but when she answered his call, she sounded like an overly excited twentysomething.

"Doing fine, Sharon, but I was calling to see if you could help me out."

"Oh, yeah? What's in it for me?" she teased, but the way she spoke made him wonder if she was actually trying to flirt.

He couldn't remember if she was in a relationship or not, but even if she wasn't, it didn't matter to him.

He cast his gaze toward Holly. Out the window of his office, he could see Holly was speaking with Valerie in the hall—it was no wonder she hadn't answered her phone. Val was being chatty, and her hands were moving wildly as she spoke. She seemed to like Holly; he recalled her chatting with her the last time they had been in the office, as well.

"I'll have to send you and your team some lunch, Sharon," he said, careful not to put himself at risk for anything that was less than professional.

"Oh, okay." Sharon sounded disappointed. "I guess that would be nice."

"Perfect." He tried not to take any pride in his gentle letdown of the woman, but in his younger years he would have fed right into her advance. "In the meantime, I need to get all the data from GAIA on the other night's SAR mission involving the missing skier."

"Okay," she said, but there was a question in her voice. "Anything you're looking for specifically?"

"I just need to see the areas our teams went and get a little more data on Moose's last location."

"Oh," Sharon said, as if she had suddenly remembered she was flirting with the dead man's best friend. "I'm so sorry about what happened."

"I appreciate that." He cut her off from going any further down that rabbit hole. He didn't want to talk to her about it. "I'll be in the office for a few more minutes, so if you need anything call, but I'll look forward to getting an email with the information."

"Absolutely," she said. "I'm here to help, Ty—in any way I can."

She couldn't help herself.

"Thanks." He hung up the phone and stood up from his desk.

He needed out of this dungeon.

For the first time since Moose's death, he finally started to feel like he was getting closer to answers—even if the answers weren't what he wanted them to be.

He had to hope Valerie wasn't complicit in his death and one of their own wouldn't have acted in such a way. But there were any number of reasons that something could have gone awry and led to this outcome; especially if they had spent time together between the sheets.

And there. Right there...was another reason he couldn't fall for Holly. Relationships only brought disaster.

He walked out into the hallway and Holly looked up at him with a smile. "How's it going in there? Do you need my help?"

"Doing fine. Actually, I need to chat with Valerie for a bit." He nodded in her direction across the bullpen. "What were you guys chatting about?"

Holly shrugged. "Nothing in particular. She was asking how the investigation was going with Robert's death and if you'd found anything interesting."

Her asking was interesting. As the evidence tech, she had access to pretty much everything he did—at least, everything that had been documented. In fact, she had likely even been on that crime scene while helping to retrieve evidence and had written the evidentiary report.

"Did she say anything about Moose?"

Holly looked at him with a questioning expression. "No. Why?"

"I'm curious, that's all." He tried to sound unconcerned.

He caught Valerie's eye and waved her over to his office before turning back to Holly. "This shouldn't take long. Then we can maybe get out of here. It's going to be a long day." He let out a long exhale as Valerie strode over toward them, weaving between the desks and the chairs that lined the hallway.

"Good luck," Holly said with a smile.

He would need more than luck—he would need a crystal ball.

Valerie made her way into his office, closing the door behind her. He sat down and waited for her to get comfortable. This was one conversation he wasn't looking forward to in the slightest.

"How are you doing with everything, Valerie?" He tented his fingers as he looked at her.

She instinctively looked down at her hands. "I'm not gonna lie, I've been better. Moose's death was really hard on me."

Though he was aware that this was a great moment for him to ask her questions about the nature of her relationship with him, he didn't feel the need to push it. She was being honest about her feelings, and he had to respect that. So instead of saying anything, he waited in silence.

"I'm sure you're not aware, but Moose and I were a lot closer than we let on." There was a crack in her voice that made him hurt for her.

Though he'd assumed that they had been in a physical relationship, he wondered if she and Moose had fallen in love. Seeing her reaction and hearing her speak, it was clear it could have been nothing else.

"He and I had been dating for about the last six months. We had been keeping it very low-key, we both knew that we were playing with fire by dating within the office." She picked at her fingernails.

He wanted to tell her that their assumption had been right. And they had been correct in not making their relationship public. Something like that would have been blood in the water. At least when it came to the gossip mill. Additionally, she would have probably been hit with an abundance of cautionary tales about Moose and his penchant for dating around.

No doubt, she knew all the rumors without anyone telling her. The amazing part was that she had still chosen to be with Moose.

He didn't know if he felt sorry for her, or if he liked her more for her ability to see past Moose's fun-seeking decisions for the great man he was. He could get how someone would have loved Moose; he'd loved the gregarious guy, as well.

"Did Moose know Holly, at all?"

Valerie looked at him, slightly confused. "No. I don't think he even saw her in person before."

The knot in his stomach loosened slightly. At the very least, Holly held no real connection to his friend and as such, no motivation to kill.

"Did you know where Moose was on the mountain on the day he was murdered?" Ty asked.

She shook her head. "I knew he was out there, running the middle line. However, that was about as close as we had come to working together that day. While we had been dating, we had been really careful not to work together in situations that could have later been picked apart by an attorney. It was one of the things that we promised each other, in an effort to avoid any potential conflicts professionally."

"That was smart." Ty thought about his burgeoning relationship with Holly. Maybe if they were careful things didn't have to go poorly.

"We really did try to avoid problems. Had I thought that anything like this would have happened while we were together..." She started to cry.

He avoided looking back at the windows where he knew Holly was watching.

"I can understand how you guys got together. I'm not here to judge you for that. However, I do need to ask you some really important questions about your relationship and your life together. Are you okay with that?"

"Are you asking as a friend, or as a detective?" She looked at him questioningly.

"Unfortunately, it's going to have to be as both."

She nodded with understanding. "Then let me clearly state that I had nothing to do with his death."

"I can appreciate that. Just make sure that you don't go

anywhere without letting me or Detective Stowe know. We don't wanna create any misunderstandings."

And just like that his interview with her was over and a whole new world of potential scenarios opened up, but one of his main concerns had subsided—Holly wasn't Moose's killer.

Chapter Seventeen

It felt like a wild goose chase. Was this what it was always like doing his job?

For a second Holly wondered if it grew tedious, but then she thought better of it. Even though the circumstances were less than ideal, he seemed to love what he was doing. That was, she assumed so, right up until the point when Valerie left his office.

She looked battle worn and exhausted. Instead of going back to her desk, Valerie made her way out of the office, closing the door behind her. Had she been sent home?

Holly couldn't hear anything that was said in the office with the door closed, but she wished she could have.

When Ty walked out a few minutes later, he looked as ravaged by whatever had been said behind those doors as Valerie did. For a moment, he stood beside Holly, staring vacantly into space as if he barely registered that she was there.

"Are you okay?" Holly asked, worried.

He nodded, but he couldn't seem to find his voice.

"What happened in there?" she pressed.

"Detective Stowe is going to have his hands full."

She didn't know what he meant, but she didn't get the impression he wanted to tell her anything else.

"I think I'm done for the day," he said, looking down at his watch. "Do you want to get an early dinner?"

She was surprised. He'd been running on empty and going nonstop for days and after this meeting he was ready to hang up his hat. It must have gone far worse than she had even assumed.

"Sure."

"Is it okay if I cook? I have some steaks and stuff." He sounded tired as he started to make his way out of the office and toward the exit.

"Ty, if you need some rest, I can go home." The last thing she wanted to do was to become a burden.

He shook his head. "You are very welcome at my place, and I want you there. I'm sorry if I'm *off*, it's not you. I just need to come to terms with a few things."

She didn't press and they walked in silence to the truck. He helped her in. When he drove, he reached out and motioned for her hand. It was such a simple thing, but it pulled at her heart as she thought about the fact that he was turning to her for comfort.

She was dying to know what all had transpired in that office, but at the same time she was glad she didn't. If it was wearing on him as much as it seemed to be, then she couldn't imagine how she would take whatever it was that he knew. He was normally so strong and so put together that seeing him like this hurt her.

The conversation had to do with Moose, and she knew that Stowe had said that there were rumors that he and Valerie had been an item. From what she could infer, that must have been chatted about—and found to be true.

Maybe that had a bad effect on Valerie's job and Ty had been forced to let her go. Yet, that didn't make sense. As it turned out, their relationship was no longer problematic—unless it had somehow resulted in the man's death.

Was that why Ty was so upset? Had Valerie played a role in the murder?

No, it wasn't possible, or she wouldn't have walked out of the office—she would have been arrested.

The truth was the gray area in the middle, no doubt, and it was understandable as to why Ty was acting as he was.

She would be there for him tonight, though. As questionable as their relationship was, and how much it was starting on shaky ground, she wasn't going to leave him when he needed support the most. Besides, just because they were going to have dinner at his place, it didn't mean that they were going to take their relationship further. In fact, she doubted that was what he had implied by inviting her. He needed away, and he needed a friend.

If history was to repeat itself when it came to their time together, she didn't have to worry about anything happening—he always had a way of running away when they grew closer.

She gripped his hand tighter, like her simple hold could make him stay or at least understand that when he ran away all it did was hurt them. She wasn't going anywhere and if he just stopped running, he would see that she wanted the world with him.

He pulled into his driveway and showed her into the house. He took out the steaks from the fridge and moved around his kitchen with an easy grace.

She glanced around her as he worked. He had a charming home. It was small and tidy and what a Realtor would have called "quaint." Yet, for both of their lifestyles it was perfect. From where she stood in the small kitchen, she could see into his living room and the small dining alcove. There was a hallway and three doors. Overall, she guessed the place to be about fifteen hundred square feet maximum.

There were a few paintings on the walls of mountains, deer and elk, the kind that she had seen sold at the ranch supply store just down the road from her clinic. One of them was strikingly similar to the moose picture that sat as the centerpiece in her office's lobby.

They really were more alike than she had thought.

"Have you always lived here by yourself?" As she spoke, she realized that she really didn't know that much about his past since the time he had exited her life.

He nodded. "I bought this place from a friend around the time I started working for the sheriff's department. It was my first big adult purchase, you know." A smile finally returned to his features.

She was relieved that she had managed to help him relax and think of something else than his meeting. "Moose helped me move everything in from my apartment. He'd come over from Helena. At the time, he was married to a nurse working over there." And his smile disappeared.

She didn't want to tell him how sorry she was about Moose again; no doubt he'd been hearing a lot of that and not just from her. Guilt would ride within her forever about his friend's death. The best she could do, and the most she could hope for now, was to catch his killer, and help Ty with his grief.

"Even though he had his share of faults, he really was a good friend. I always knew that if I needed anything, I could call him. He'd show up rain or shine. It was why I was so on board with him coming to work at the station.

I even talked to the sheriff for him, in an effort to help him get the job. When he was hired, it was one of the best days of our lives. We got to be *Starsky and Hutch* all over again."

This was about the most she had ever heard him speak. And she was glad that he was finding some catharsis with her.

He grabbed a pan out of the cabinet and put it on the burner, letting it heat up. "I didn't go to the bars like he did. I know too many people so going out can be exhausting— everyone wants to chat and I try to keep my work at work— but I never really chastised him for going out and wanting to be social. It was his life, and he had been through one heck of a divorce."

An idea popped into her head. "Do you think that his ex had anything to do with his death?"

Ty shook his head. "I don't think that Tracy would have sprung for the gas to come over and do it. She didn't like him, and they had a lot of pent-up hostility toward each other, but I don't think that either one of them hated the other so much that they would have turned to murder. Besides, if she was going to do that, she would have probably done it during the divorce proceedings."

That made more sense. She knew she was scratching in the dirt.

He threw the steaks on the pan, and they started to sizzle. After a couple of moments, the smell of roasting garlic, beef and spices filled the air. Her mouth watered.

"You know, I don't remember the last time a man made a meal for me." She moved to the small kitchen alcove, which hosted a two-person table. It was the cheap kind with a chipped melamine top and black plastic legs. The two chairs didn't match, and when she sat in hers it wobbled slightly.

"Well, I don't remember the last time I cooked for a woman." He smiled at her. "Be careful on that chair, it's a bit like riding a bronc. You wanna use two hands to stay on." He chuckled.

The sound of his laugh made her pulse quicken. She couldn't recall if she'd heard him laugh in the last few days, but if she had her way, she'd have loved to hear it every day.

He grabbed a couple of potatoes and tossed them in the microwave. She noticed that he had punched far too few holes in them, but she wasn't about to critique his cooking. She simply appreciated it for what it was, an act of kindness.

She'd heard people talk about their love languages in her office, quite regularly. Usually, it was women talking about their partners giving them massages and how their love language was touch. While she appreciated a good back rub or hand holding, what she had always loved most in a relationship was a man who performed acts of service. She was always in so much control and doing and going a thousand different directions that it was nice to be taken care of on occasion. However, she hadn't been pursued by a man seriously in over a year—with the exception of Robert's continuous advances.

Even now, dead, Robert was still trying to ruin her chances for love.

She really did hate the man.

"Are you doing okay with everything?" he asked, looking over at her and apparently reading her like a book.

She nodded, but it was met with a look of disbelief from him.

Apparently, they were both going to talk about their feelings. She'd not had a safe space in which to open up to anyone in so many years that she was a little uncomfortable with the idea. In the past, whatever she had told Robert in passing at work, he had always used it as ammunition to hurt her later. It was opening up to him and allowing him to believe they were anything other than colleagues that had caused the situation that had transpired.

"I'm better than I should be in some ways," she said, thinking about her grief—or lack thereof—when it came to Robert. "And in others, I will never forgive myself." She stared at the chip on the corner of the table. "I'm just going to have to learn to live with it all, though. There's nothing I can change."

He started the microwave with a series of beeps, made sure the steaks were on low, rinsed off his hands, and then walked over to her and sat down. He reached across the table and took her hands in his. "Moose's death…" He paused like he was struggling to find the right words. "I don't know what happened, or who killed him, but it didn't happen because of anything you did or didn't do."

She looked up at him and stared into his striking brown eyes. He really was handsome, so handsome that in this moment she almost felt like she was staring into the sun, and she was forced to look away.

"What if everything that happened so far *was* because of me? What if Robert was the one who killed Moose?"

He was surprised by her query. "He could have, but why? He had no motive. But even on the off chance he did, it still wouldn't make anything that happened out there your responsibility or fault."

How had he already thought about this being a possibility, while it was earth-shatteringly new to her? In moments like this, it was no wonder he was a detective. He'd found his calling.

"Do you always have all the answers?" she asked, making sure to smile as she teased him.

He shrugged slightly, then let go of her hands and leaned back in the chair. "What can I say? I'm an overthinker."

"I can tell," she said, smiling. "I always knew you were, but I have to say that I think you've gotten better at it over the years."

"Better at it?" He smiled but quirked an eyebrow as he looked at her. "Normally, overthinking isn't what most people would consider a good quality. It leads to problems in relationships sometimes. I'm always wanting to know that the person I'm with is safe and cared for and it can come across like a red flag."

She could see how a woman would think it was. "Are you controlling?"

"Absolutely not, or I try not to be. I've just been at this job long enough that I am protective of the people I care about. Overly so, really. I'm always working on it."

She didn't think that a man taking an active interest in her welfare was overreaching or a negative, but then again, she wasn't looking for the same kind of relationships that she had experienced while young and naive. As an adult, she would expect her partner to be open and aboveboard and request the same considerations from her.

She put her hand out on the table. "None of us are perfect. We all have our idiosyncrasies. My only real dealbreaker, besides the obvious, is if a man refuses to grow and change. I want to be with someone who is always striving to be better for me and makes me want to strive to be the best I can be for him."

"Do you think you can be with an overthinker, though? They say we need the world's best communicators in order for relationships to work." He sent her a dazzling smile.

The warmth of it soaked into her heart and made her lighten. "I'd like to think I don't have a communication problem—I think the last few days can act as a testament to my ability to work through tough situations."

"But what about overthinking?"

She smiled. "Did you just overthink my response?" She giggled. "I can handle it all."

He stood up and moved to her. He lifted her chin with his finger and gave her a soft kiss on the lips. He pulled back and stared into her eyes. "Did I ever tell you how beautiful I think you are? How beautiful you've always been?"

She swooned. There was nothing like the most handsome man she'd ever known telling her she was beautiful. She couldn't help the giggle which escaped her lips. "You already got me to your house, you don't have to lay it on so thick."

He kept holding the side of her face, stroking her hairline gently with his thumb as he looked upon her. "I'd hate to think of the type of men you've been with if you think I'm not being truthful, or that I'm trying to get in your pants. I have a terrible habit of saying exactly what I mean. However, if you're game, I'd be happy to prove to you exactly how beautiful I think you are."

Heat rose in her cheeks, and she fidgeted in the wobbly chair, making it squeak loudly on the floor. "Oh," she said, embarrassed by both his candor and her reaction. "That was one heck of a pickup line." She fanned herself.

He threw his head back in a laugh. "Fair enough, that last part was a little bit close to the line of wanting to get in your pants, but can you blame a guy?"

She was sincerely surprised by his forwardness. Of all the ways she thought tonight would go, this hadn't been on the list. "Do you really want to *be* with me? You've been so hot and cold with me—you know, like the other night when you disappeared from my house. Until you texted, I was actually worried about you."

He dropped his head in shame. "I apologize for that. I do. I… It's just been a long couple of weeks—for both of us. I didn't want to muddle things between us."

"But you are okay with taking that next step now?" She gently grazed her lips where he had touched hers. "I mean, I know that my stopping this isn't sexy, and I love being kissed, but I just want to make sure that you are thinking clearly."

He ran his hand against the back of his neck and sighed. After a second of awkward silence, he stood up and made his way over to the stove. He moved the steaks around, like they needed his full attention.

"It is ridiculous of me to want you, but the heart wants what the heart wants."

"It's ridiculous?" she countered, a pang of agony shooting through her.

"You're right, on paper *we* are a bad idea. We have already tried it once—"

"We were young, and you broke up with me," she argued, not letting him finish.

"Okay, but I didn't break up with you—you broke up with me." He smiled. "But besides that, we are going to come under the microscope. Detective Stowe already thinks we are an item, and he is going to be asking a ton of questions."

"If he already thinks we are, then what is the difference? If we are going to be judged…" She paused. "Wait, your private life is your private life. You wouldn't be the first person to have a relationship in this town or in your department. Big Sky is a small town, everyone is connected in one way or another."

He put his hand up, not bothering to argue.

"Which means that there has to be something else—" An idea struck her. "Hold up, you don't think I had anything to do with any of this? Some small part of you that is worried?"

He looked at her with a wide-eyed expression, almost like he'd been caught. "I don't, now."

She gasped. He'd told her not to feel like any of this was her fault, that she couldn't take the blame and yet, when she pushed with hard questions, she had found the truth—he thought she was in some way responsible. She should have known.

She stood up from the rickety chair and moved to leave. There was no way she could stand one more second in this man's presence. He had lied to her.

He grabbed her by the wrist, not so hard as to be threatening but with just enough pressure to hold her back from running.

He clicked the stove off. "Wait. Don't go. I don't want you to go."

"That's not what I asked," she countered, her lips trembling with anger and hurt.

"I don't think you had anything to do with it. But something had been bothering me. I have a strange question…"

There was a look of trepidation as he looked at her. "This morning, when I was in your house, I noticed something."

"Okay…"

"There was a butcher knife missing from your knife block."

She let out a long, annoyed huff. "What does that have to do with…" She stopped herself. That kind of knife had likely been used to kill Moose. "But you know I was nowhere near Moose. I didn't have anything to do with his death."

"I know and that's why I didn't say anything then, but it's been bothering me since I noticed it. Do you know where that knife is?" He looked at her as if he were begging.

She shook her head. "I didn't even know it was missing. And I don't remember the last time I used the knives in my kitchen. I'm the queen of takeout and cheese sandwiches."

"So, you don't know how long it could have been gone? Has anyone else been in your house, besides me, that you know about?" He pulled her closer to him and he sat down and moved to have her sit on his lap.

She hesitated, still angry that he hadn't told her how he was feeling or what he was thinking before this. If he had just brought it up, they could have solved this and things between them would have been easier.

"I have no idea, but I hope you know that I'm not hiding anything from you, and I never want you to think that I was capable of something like murder." It tore at her that he would have even contemplated it for a second. However, he had to have known it wasn't in her nature or he would have said something before.

"I know, and I've always known that." He pulled at her, and as he did, she felt herself forgive him.

She gave in to him, sitting down on his lap. She could never really be mad at this man. He had such a way of calming the storm within her. She'd never met anyone who had the ability to do that for her. That had to mean something.

He reached up and cupped her face gently. "Look at me," he said softly. She did as he asked. "I want you. And I need you to know that no matter what happens, I'm in your corner. Do you want to be with me? If you don't want me, I understand."

She melted and she leaned into him, putting her forehead against his. "Ty, I've always wanted you. There's never been a question about that."

He pulled her in, taking her lips with his.

He kissed her in a way she had forgotten even existed. It was deep and charged, silently speaking of wants and desires, and the kind that made promises. She spread her lips open as the kiss deepened and they grew hungrier, their tongues moving faster and more manic.

"Ty... I want you..." she whispered into his mouth. "I want you inside of me."

He stood up, helping her to wrap her legs around him. He sat her on the top of the table. "I want you, too. I want you *now*."

She reached down, feeling how badly he wanted her. Her body was aching for him. She unzipped his pants, stroking him over his smooth boxers. He was so big. Her mouth watered for him.

He kissed down her neck, cupping her breasts in his hand as he swept his kiss lower along the edge of her shirt collar. He reached down, pulling at the bottom of her shirt. He stopped kissing her just long enough to pull her shirt over her head before burying his face between the creamy mounds of her breasts.

He moaned as he kissed along her pink bra and he pushed back the fabric, exposing her pink nipple. He pulled it into his mouth, sucking on it until it was hard and tender, the sensation of his tongue flipping against her nipples made her pulse race.

She pulled at his pants clumsily until he reached down and unbuttoned them and let them fall to the floor. He reached for her and slipped her pants down her waist, kissing her stomach and down to her panties as he pulled her pants off and freed her.

He ran his tongue over the top of her panties, making her gasp and moan at the sensation of his mouth on her.

That. Feeling. It was so…amazing.

He pushed her panties to the side as he took more of her into his mouth. He flicked his tongue against her, then sucked. The sensation drove her to the edge of madness as he repeated it again and again. She threw her head back as he pressed his chin against her and flicked.

"I'm so…" But as she was about to say the last word, the wave of ecstasy crashed over her, and she called out with pleasure.

He sped up, working her until she was quivering and sensitive. "Stop…" she begged.

He leaned back with a smile on his face. Wetness covered his chin.

"Let me kiss you," she said, barely able to move.

He leaned over and she tasted herself on him. She licked her juices from his lips, and he moaned into her mouth.

Weak and shaky, she stepped back from the table and

dropped to her knees in front of him, pulling down his boxers. "Now," she said, smiling up at him as they looked into each other's eyes. "It's my turn."

Chapter Eighteen

Last night had been, hands down, the best night of his life. Ty had assumed that if he got a chance to have Holly in his bed again that it would have been incredible, but the reality was so much better than anything he could have imagined.

At one point, she'd begged him to bend her over the table. That was one memory that he would never forget. If anything, he hoped that they could re-create that on a regular basis.

That was, assuming that they were something more than a onetime thing.

He picked up his phone on the kitchen counter beside him as he stared longingly at the melamine table where so much had happened last night. He loved and hated that table. Taking his cup of coffee and his phone, he walked over to the table and gave it a light shove.

In their play, the thing had been tested to the max. It moved and swayed as he pushed against it. He would need to fix it and strengthen it if they were going to keep doing as they had.

He smiled at the thought. He would buy stronger mounting brackets for the tabletop as soon as he got the chance. Or maybe he just needed a table with four sturdy legs.

As he thought about his options, his phone buzzed with an email, and it pulled him from his planning.

He took a sip of his coffee and put it on the table before opening up his email. Both the ME and the mapping tech, Sharon, had sent him notes. According to her findings, everyone on the mountain had been exactly where they had stated—or, at least, their tracking equipment had been

He clicked on the ME's note. They had finally managed to get the toxicology reports back from Moose's body. No foreign substances had been found. As for Robert, he'd been taking large amounts of opiates. The sedatives had only been slightly metabolized in his system—meaning that he had taken a downer in the hour or so before his death.

That was odd.

The first opioid that came to mind was fentanyl. He wasn't sure which class of drugs physical therapists had access to, but he would make sure to ask Holly as soon as she woke up.

If Robert was abusing fentanyl, it helped to make some sense of his erratic behavior. It was far more potent than heroin or morphine and just as addictive. Often, people who took fentanyl had instances of hallucinations and auditory and visual disturbances.

What was strange was that Robert had been working. It was shocking that he could be a professional by day and an addict by night.

Then again, he had seen this kind of thing many times before. Addicts came in every socioeconomic bracket. No one was immune.

He looked at the numbers. According to the report, the amount in his system wasn't enough to cause an overdose. The ME had updated the report, and the immediate cause of death was listed as a gunshot wound to the lower mandible, exiting through the top of the skull. They had left the manner of death unselected.

They were waiting for his investigation. He would need to call them. It seemed entirely too possible that it was suicide, but there was something about the entire situation with Robert and Moose that made him question everything.

He pulled up the pictures he'd taken in Robert's master bedroom where they had located his body. He stared at the first image of Robert's head. He zoomed in on the man's chin, staring at the tattooing the gunshot had made on his skin. It was dark and heavy around the wound and the barrel had even burned his flesh, which meant the gun had been pressed directly against the skin when the trigger was pulled.

According to the report, they had found gunshot residue, or GSR, on Robert's left hand, but that simply meant he was in the room at the time of the shooting. What surprised him was that they had noted that there was no obvious residue on the right hand where he would have been holding the gun to inflict such a wound.

He looked back at his phone and the picture of the Glock 19. It was on the ground near Robert's right hand. From the picture it appeared as though the moment he had died his arm and hand had gone limp and the gun had been dropped. It was consistent with most suicides he had seen in the past.

He zoomed in on the image. Something was a little off. He couldn't pinpoint what was strange about it, but there was *something* about the gun's placement that didn't feel right.

He clicked on the other pictures of the gun. From some of the angles, he could see where blood had sprayed back on the gun and dried to the hot barrel. It was undoubtedly the gun used in the shooting, though they hadn't run ballistics on the bullet they had pulled from the ceiling above the body.

As he zoomed in on the last picture, taken from near the level of the gun, he realized what was bothering him. The grip of the gun was slightly under the man's thigh.

If he had shot himself, it wasn't impossible, but it was unlikely that the body would have been atop the weapon.

He stared at the picture and scrolled through the rest in his phone. He had no idea how he had missed this on scene. However, it was barely under his body.

Then again, maybe the body had relaxed after death and moved slightly or perhaps it was an effect of rigor or some death process, which had caused the gun to appear beneath the man's thigh.

Maybe it had something to do with the fentanyl in his system.

Or perhaps he just didn't want to accept that Robert had killed himself. In a secret dark part of his brain, he hated the idea that the man had taken the easy way out of his life after he had caused so much upheaval in Holly's.

"Good morning," Holly said, pulling him from his thoughts.

He was as grateful as he was sure that those thoughts were probably some indicators that he needed therapy.

"Hi, babe," he said, shutting off his phone and shoving it in his pocket.

She looked adorable with her mussed hair and sleepy expression. He handed her his cup of coffee. "Here, you can have mine. I'll make another."

He gave her a peck on her forehead as she took the coffee from him.

"Thank you," she said, her voice hoarse. "Is everything all right? You seem *off.*"

He started to make himself another cup. "Because I gave you my coffee? Yeah, I see how you could get there." He knew exactly what she was talking about, but he was a little surprised that she could so easily pick up his emotions without him saying anything.

"Not because of the coffee. Did I do something wrong last night?" Her face was dead serious.

He realized his misstep. "It's nothing like that, I promise. I never want you to think that. Last night was perfect." He pulled her into his arms and kissed her lips. "You're perfect."

She burrowed deeper into his embrace, and he tightened his hold. A man could get used to this. He'd forgotten how good it felt to have a woman in his life whom he cared about.

"I'm far from perfect, but I'm glad you had fun."

He had a hell of a lot more than some fun.

If he had his way, he would be honored to call her perfect every single day.

"Maybe we can repeat it tonight?" he offered, a sly smirk on his face.

She giggled and the sound vibrated against his chest. He loved that feeling.

The vibrating intensified and as it stopped and started again, he realized it was coming from his back pocket. It forced him out of their embrace as he answered it. It was Detective Stowe.

"How's it going, Stowe?" he answered, slightly annoyed

that the man had interrupted what was a great moment—and long awaited.

"It's going well. I was calling about the Robert Finch case. Do you have a moment?"

He grabbed his coffee. He was going to need a bigger cup. "What's up?"

"I got the phone records back from Robert Finch. I just wanted to give you a heads-up that I'm going to send them your way."

"Perfect. Did you get the ME reports? See the fentanyl?"

Stowe chuckled, dryly. "Our boy was definitely using. He had some major amounts in his blood. He'd obviously been using for a while."

Holly's eyebrows rose in surprise, making him realize he had yet to tell her about what they'd found. "That's what I got, too. Still not a factor in his death, though." He cleared his throat. "Did you notice that the gun used was sitting slightly under his thigh?"

"I did," Stowe said. "I have been looking into similar cases. So far, I've only found a couple that had matching scenarios and results. The only time they've had something like this has been when a body has been left in the heat and there's been swelling with decomposition, or if a body has been disturbed."

"Well, that or it was never really a suicide and the murderer screwed up," Ty added.

"I went there, too." Stowe paused. "They pulled prints from the gun, but they were pretty poor quality. I think someone wiped it."

Ty pulled in a breath.

"Yep, exactly," Stowe said, must having heard him. "I'm going to see if we can pull any prints from the brass."

"Let me know how it turns out."

"You got it, and I'm sending you the phone records. Let me know if anything stands out."

"Did you see anything of note?" Ty asked, looking at his phone for a second, looking to see if Stowe had sent him the records.

There was nothing.

"Actually, on his apps, it looks like he was spending a lot of his time looking into Holly Dean."

The news didn't come as a surprise. "Anybody else?" Ty asked, his gaze moving to Holly. He could tell she was listening in.

"There are a few other women it appeared he had been speaking to, but I don't know any of them personally. That's where I was hoping you'll come in and use your local knowledge." Stowe paused. "Also, I was hoping to talk to your evidence tech about Robert's body placement. What is their name?"

"No problem. That's Valerie Keller. She's in the office today, I believe." He didn't add in the part about her being hard to contact on the phone sometimes.

"Great, I'll stop by. I'll be in touch."

As he hung up the phone, he looked over at Holly, who was taking a drink of her coffee. She had a contemplative expression on her face.

"Are you okay? I realize this has to be hard on you," he said, concerned that his conversation may have been the reason she looked as she did.

She sat her coffee cup down on the kitchen counter and looked over at him. "Actually, I was thinking about the conversation I last had with Valerie. Or, I guess it wasn't the last conversation, but when I first met her." She stared off into space as she must have been thinking about it.

"She actually mentioned that she had a sister who had been dating Robert."

"What?" he asked, shocked. "She never mentioned it to me."

"Well, it's not like she was dating him and at this point who wasn't Robert dating? Seriously, he was even dating Penny from the PT clinic." She forced a laugh, and it sounded almost painful.

His phone pinged with a message from the detective. He opened up the email and clicked on the attachment, which contained a comprehensive report of Robert's phone activity. According to the data, Robert had called Holly 147 times since his last billing cycle three weeks ago. In total Robert had made nearly 300 phone calls, many of them to the number he recognized belonged to the physical therapy clinic. There were only 47 phone calls which weren't somehow related to Holly.

The man was definitely a stalker.

The numbers for his text messages were of a similar ratio. However, it appeared that he had been in contact with at least two dozen individuals. His social media was interesting. He'd spent a great deal of time on one particular platform, which was photo based. There, he had been searching "girl next door," "hot physical therapists" and "how to make a woman fall for you," amongst a variety of other terms.

He really didn't like him. None of what he was finding surprised him. The guy was pathetic and a confirmed drug addict.

Holly stepped to his side, and he held out his phone so she could take a peek at the list, as well. She scanned through the pages, stopping on his messages.

"Is there a page where we can see who all these numbers belonged to?" she asked, pointing at the phone numbers he had been in contact with.

"We can pull them up on NCIC. It's the national database law enforcement uses. It basically has everything about everyone. It's actually a bit terrifying how much data is in that thing." He had used it to look into Robert when he'd been digging around after his death, but the man didn't have any real record when it came to criminal activities. As for his private information, he'd learned about every apartment and phone number Robert had ever had, as well as all of his family members' addresses and phone numbers.

"I've heard about it."

A sense of excitement filled him. They weren't any closer to finding answers to Robert's death, but at least they were getting some more information. He closed his phone and stuffed it in his back pocket. He walked toward the door and put his hand on the doorknob. "I'm going to run out and grab my computer. I left it in my pickup. We can sit down and dig into these numbers. I don't think it will take us too long to come up with the names."

She gave him a strange look, one that almost hinted at fear. Was she worried about being left alone? Her enemy was dead.

He stopped and came back to her, not wanting to see that expression on her face ever again. It pained him to see her in pain. He took her into his embrace, and he dropped his hands down to her lower back as he looked into her eyes. "Everything is going to be okay. You are safe. You will always be safe with me, babe."

She relaxed in his arms and laid her head against his chest as though she was taking a moment to listen to his heart. As she did, his heart started to ache and he wished, not for the first time, that he could get even closer to her even though they were already touching. It was an illogical thought, but it made him realize exactly how much this woman meant to him.

He was the luckiest man on the planet to be holding a woman like her in his arms. He never wanted to let her go.

After a long moment, she leaned back and looked up at him, waiting for his kiss. He obliged, moving down and giving her a kiss that he hoped she recognized as standing for something far more real and more tangible than simply lust.

She smiled, her mouth still against his, and it made him wonder if she read his kiss for exactly what he had intended. "Go grab your computer," she said, her breath warm against his lips.

He couldn't say he really wanted to go anywhere, but he let her go. He hurried outside, and as he did, he realized he wasn't wearing any shoes when his feet touched the fresh snow on the ground.

"Oh...damn," he said between gasping breaths.

He took out his keys and unlocked his pickup as he hurried through the icy snow. His feet ached with the cold by the time he reached his rig. As he opened the door, he watched as his breath made a cloud in the air in front of him.

It was barely in the single digits outside, if even that. It would have been perfect weather for being on the sled in the mountains; the snow would be great for riding. If Moose had still been alive, he would have been getting a call this morning to hit the slopes.

He really was going to miss his friend.

Thinking about Moose, he needed to reach out to Rebecca and make sure she was doing okay. She was probably having a really hard time right now, planning the funeral and waiting for the ME to release his remains to the funeral home. He felt so bad for her.

He moved to grab his computer, but as he did, he caught sight of the empty spot where he normally parked his work rig. That round had nearly cost him his life. Any of them could have—and that was to say nothing about Holly. She had gotten down in the pickup, taken cover, but that didn't always mean that a person wouldn't take a hit.

They were both lucky to still be alive.

He'd already lost Moose; he couldn't lose another person who he cared about.

And whoever had shot at them...they were still out there. Moreover, they had probably been the ones behind Moose's death.

He picked up his computer and slid it under his arm as he shut the pickup door. His feet were so cold now that the snow around them was melting, but slowly and as it did it left fat droplets of cold water on his steadily reddening skin.

He needed to get back inside and to Holly.

Though he couldn't explain it, a strange sense of foreboding and fear filled him.

He glanced around toward the front of the house, but he was alone out here in the wintery morning. He hated that ugly wiggling feeling that started in his stomach and climbed up to his heart and made it race. It was akin to fear, and he'd only felt it a handful of times before, unless he was under fire or in direct fight or flight.

Something was wrong, but he just couldn't put his finger on it. It reminded him of the feeling he had gotten when he discovered that the gun had been accidentally moved under Robert's leg.

Had the body or the gun been tampered with? The thought dawned on him.

But he and Stowe were the first on scene. And he knew that they hadn't touched the gun. Which opened up the possibility that someone had been at that potential crime scene before they had—but whether someone had a role in Robert's death or if they had just disturbed the scene was a question of its own.

He walked around the side of the house and toward his garage. Just like the other night at Holly's house, the garage light was on.

Strange. I didn't park there last night. He looked out at his truck, which was parked in front of the garage door. If he remembered correctly, they hadn't even walked through the garage to get inside and last night the light definitely hadn't been turned on.

The fear in him roiled to something more, something resembling the tingling of burgeoning anger. Someone had been in there—or maybe they still were.

He reached down to his waist where his gun normally rested on his hip. He didn't feel his holster and realized that he was only wearing jeans and a shirt—he hadn't gotten ready for work, and he hadn't put on his gun to come out and get his computer.

His feet were burning now; they were so cold in the snow that they had started to once again feel warm. He knew the dangers that came with the sensation, but he couldn't worry about his feet. He needed to know who had been in his garage and why.

Stepping quietly, he made his way to the side door of the structure and slowly twisted the door handle. "Put your hands up!" he yelled, slamming open the door.

There was no one in his direct line of sight as he

glanced through the opening, careful to keep his body behind cover in case someone decided to open fire.

"Get down on the ground and put your hands on the back of your head!" he ordered, as if there was a perpetrator inside listening to him, someone he didn't see.

He cleared the entrance and glanced inside. The place was filled with stacks of boxes, a table saw, router, lathe and his tool bench. There was only silence. He moved inside, carefully crouching down to see if someone was hiding under his old '68 Charger he'd always planned on refinishing.

He was alone.

This place was always locked up, but when he'd come through the side door, it had been open. He walked over toward the doorknob. There were fresh scratches in the brass like someone had used metal tools to clumsily pick the lock.

Everything appeared to be in its place and no boxes had been brought down from the shelves or rifled through, and if someone was looking for something of value to steal, there were plenty of expensive tools that were still sitting around. Whoever had been inside hadn't come here with the intention of robbing him. So, why would they have broken in?

And then he spotted it. The shiny blade caught the light just right and pulled his attention. He walked over toward the mysterious knife. He'd not seen this in his garage before, but as he neared the butcher knife, he had a sinking feeling he knew where it had been.

On the black handle, he wasn't completely sure, but he thought he could see the remnants of dried blood. It was brown and crackled.

Not touching it, he backed up slowly from where he

stood and didn't touch another thing as he made his way outside. The door stood open and the lights were on, but he didn't care.

He reached into his back pocket and pulled out his phone. First, he called dispatch and let them know about the break-in, asking for the closest deputies to make their way to his residence.

Next, he texted Stowe. His message was simple. I think I may have found the murder weapon.

He didn't wait for a response. Instead, he slowly made his way back to the front of the house. Outside, leading from the road were a new set of footprints. They went straight to the door. From the distance between them and the snow they'd kicked up, the person who'd left them had been running.

He hurried to the door, his fear escalating.

He grabbed the doorknob and tried to turn it, but it didn't budge. He'd been locked out.

Chapter Nineteen

Holly was puttering around in the kitchen, looking for bacon in the freezer, when she heard the front door slam closed and the lock click into place.

"I'm going to cook us a little breakfast. I'm thinking eggs, hash browns, bacon?" she asked, not really expecting an answer.

She hummed as she found the bacon and took it to the sink. She turned on the water and let the liquid pour over the frozen meat as she removed it from the plastic. She set it on the cutting board and went back to the freezer. She pulled out a bag of frozen hash browns.

The song "Good Morning, Beautiful" was stuck in her head and she danced as she sang random words between humming. She had always liked country music. As she thought about music, she wondered what kind of music Ty liked. She didn't really remember what they had been listening to in his truck when they had been together when they'd been younger. Her mind had always been on him.

After last night, she held no doubts that she would love to get the chance to be by his side more often. Daily. No, *hourly* would be best. Bottom line, no amount of him would ever be enough.

She smiled widely as she thought about his tongue on her and the way he felt when he was between her thighs.

She had found everything she had been missing in her life, and he had basically been right down the street these last few years.

If only she hadn't been so wrapped up in the chaos and drama of her life, maybe she would have found him before.

There was a slam against the front door, and then the pounding of fists.

"Holly! Get out of there!" Ty's voice sounded through the front door.

She stopped, unsure if she was hearing him right.

What happened? Why was he so upset?

She stared at the door as though she had been hearing things.

The picture on the wall near the door swayed as Ty pounded again. And it pulled her from her frozen response. She started to rush toward the door. "Holly! Holly, are you okay? Holly!" His voice was high and panicked.

"I'm—"

She stopped as someone grabbed her around the waist from behind. The force was incredible as the person hit the small of her back and their knee connected with the back of her thigh. Pain coursed through her, and she called out in shock and horror as her body dropped to the ground.

She screamed.

"Shut up!" a woman yelled at her as she slammed her in the ground so hard that it knocked the wind out of Holly's lungs.

She kicked behind her with her good leg, trying to roll over, but wheezing with pain.

Her lungs ached as they begged for air and her vision grew hazy. All she could see was the maple-colored floor beneath her face. She'd caught herself with her hands and as she moved, her left wrist popped, and a fire raced up her arm and into her shoulder.

She tried to call out, but without air all she could do was garble and wheeze.

A fist connected with her kidney, and she made a strange, warbled cry, which drove the last little bit of air from her. Her eyes widened, but she forced herself to fight. She had to fight.

She kicked wildly, her legs flying behind her as she struggled through the pain. She fought like a child stuck in a nightmare, flailing and striking at anything and everything. Her foot connected with soft flesh as someone grabbed her leg.

She used the leverage they provided to turn herself over.

Her eyes connected with the woman—she didn't know her. The woman had long dark hair; it was matted with what looked like blood in places and stray strands stuck out at weird angles around her gaunt, colorless face. The woman was speaking in gibberish.

She was muttering, but Holly wasn't sure if it was because the woman had also gotten the wind knocked out of her or if she was intoxicated.

"I… You…shhhhhh… I…sh…" The woman stared at her.

There was what appeared to be blood on her white shirt and down the legs of her pants, but it was brown with age. She wore a dark coat; its sleeves were covered in dirt and there were holes up and down the arms. Where there must have been a logo was a large open flap, which exposed the white cotton stuffing beneath.

The woman looked as unstable as she sounded.

"Who…" Holly said, finally managing to start to catch her breath.

The air felt sweet and cold in her aching lungs. Even in pain, she was grateful for that little bit of oxygen.

"Your worst nightmare, witch." The woman's voice came out ragged and as she spoke there was spittle spraying wildly from her lips. She tipped her head back in a manic laugh, and it caused the matted hair in the back to push up. It appeared like she almost had horns.

When she laughed, there was something Holly recognized about the woman's face. She looked like someone she knew, but she couldn't put her finger on it.

She pulled in a larger breath as the woman lunged forward. Holly kicked as hard as she could using every ounce of her strength and her foot connected with the woman's pelvis, where her zipper on her pants rested. She could feel the bite of the metal beneath her foot.

The woman dropped to her knees as she yelped in pain and grabbed at her crotch. She went down hard, making a thumping noise as she connected with the floor. Holly fisted her hand and drew it back. As she struck the woman in the stomach, she realized she'd never really punched anyone before in her life. Right now, that fact didn't matter. If anything, it gave her a strange sense of pride.

The woman grabbed at her belly, but rage filled her eyes. Holly wasn't afraid of the woman, only the fact that she was struggling to catch her breath.

As she went to strike the woman again, there was the sound of breaking glass in the living room and a rock landed on the floor a few feet from her. Glass had sprayed around the carpet, making it even more dangerous than before. Cold air filled the room and it bit at her nose.

The woman gave a low, guttural squeal and kicked Holly right in the back of the thigh as she tried to defend herself. The kick hurt but it was nothing like the pain she was feeling in her wrist.

Ty looked through the window, his face framed by the jagged, broken glass. "Don't you dare touch her!"

The woman looked at him and flipped him the bird. "You're just as bad as she is. You both deserve to die— and you will."

He looked around him like he was searching for a weapon, and as he drew away the woman's attention, Holly rose to her feet. She tucked her wrist against her body and searched the living room for something she could use. Near the couch was a lamp. The body of the lamp looked almost like a bat. It would be perfect.

She picked it up, jerking the cord from the wall.

She moved toward the woman, but as she did the woman saw her and instead of facing her in battle, she ran toward the back door.

"You're not going to get away that easy." Holly chased after the woman, wrapping the cord around the body of the lamp as she prepared to battle. "You don't get to come into this house and try to kill me."

She charged toward the door after her. Readying herself to strike.

"Just let her go," Ty ordered. "I'll go around the back. Call the police."

The back door slammed as the woman ran outside.

She stopped and stared down at the weapon in her hand.

Her left wrist was crooked, but it didn't hurt as much as it should have. She could still go after this woman.

She glanced toward Ty as he disappeared.

Call the police. I need to call the police.

Holly dropped the lamp and grabbed her phone, which was sitting on the living room table where she had left it last night.

It was dead.

You have to be kidding me. The one time I need my phone...

She ran toward the kitchen, and as she did, she spotted the knife block by the stove. As she pulled the butcher knife from the block, she couldn't help but feel some type of poetic justice. If this was the woman who had killed Moose, then this was the way she deserved to die.

Was she the kind of person who was capable of killing another?

Shadows filled her mind. If it was simply herself in danger, she didn't think she would be capable of being deadly. However, if this woman was hurting someone she loved it would be entirely different.

She rushed toward the door carrying the big knife.

No, she couldn't do as this woman had done. If she killed the woman, she was no better than the murderer.

And what if this was merely some random break-in, what if the woman had nothing to do with Moose's death?

Just because the woman appeared to be high, it didn't mean anything; it only meant that their town had a drug problem. Sure, Robert had had drugs in his system, but assuming this woman's guilt made Holly equally dangerous.

TY WAS BREATHING hard as he rounded the corner of the house and sprinted toward the woman in the distance.

He could catch her. He had to catch her. She had hurt the woman he loved.

Anger roiled through him.

He'd never thought of himself as a dangerous man, but in this moment, there was no one more deadly.

"Get down on the ground!" he ordered.

She didn't even slow down.

As he ran, he realized his computer was still under his arm. He hadn't thought of it or about it since he had grabbed it from the pickup. He considered throwing it after the woman but knew he didn't have that kind of reach.

"This is Detective Terrell with the Madison County Sheriff's Department. If you do not stop, I will be forced to shoot!" he yelled.

She didn't need to know that he wasn't carrying a gun.

The woman slowed down and as she did, he gained ground.

She looked over her shoulder, acquiring her target, which was him, before starting to run harder. His freezing feet ached as he moved into a barefooted sprint. He was so close he could almost reach her, but she was just outside of his grasp.

He remembered his computer. He hated the damn thing anyway.

He grabbed it with both hands and swung it at her as hard as he could. He hit her right on the back of the head.

She dropped.

In the distance were the sounds of police cars.

They weren't a second too soon.

Chapter Twenty

Detective Stowe was sitting in the gray hard interrogation room, staring silently at Valerie Keller. Valerie's eyes were puffy and red, and her hair was loose and unkempt. A piece jutted out from the side above her ear where she had feebly attempted to gain some control over her world. She'd failed.

In the second interrogation room, sat her sister, Evelyn. This room was even more austere with nothing more than an industrial table, complete with a loop to attach handcuffs, and two plastic chairs.

Ty hated that Valerie had gotten wrapped up in this. She was a nice person, but he was struggling to come to terms with what had taken place. She had to have been involved or at least had some knowledge of her sister's intentions, but this was her chance to tell her side of the story and exonerate herself from a potential crime.

Holly was scratching at the edge of her blue plaster cast on her left arm, and he was surprised that it was already bothering her. It was going to be a long six weeks, but he would be there to take care of her and get her everything she needed.

He felt horrible that she had been hurt in the home invasion, but he was glad that he had been there and had been able to stop the woman before she had killed Holly. Another couple of minutes, and he held no doubt that the woman would have tried to beat her to death.

He'd be lying if he didn't kind of love the fact that when he had found Holly, shaking and crying after the police had arrived at his place, that she was still holding the lamp. He'd asked her what it was about, and she'd explained that she intended to take down the woman if need be.

It was funny to him that they had both gone to household objects in order to have a weapon.

He'd always heard a computer could be his best weapon, but he had never really thought of it as one as much as he did now. The thought made a smile flutter over his lips.

When he arrived in his office this morning, there had even been a little pink toddler computer on his desk, with the note that read "In case of emergencies."

His coworkers definitely thought they were a bunch of clowns. But it did make him laugh.

On the other side of the coin, when the sheriff had called him into his office after the attack, he wasn't as amused. But he really couldn't say anything as he had used the computer to stop a crime. No doubt it would end up costing the department a couple grand, but he wasn't sad or repentant. The only thing he was sorry about was the fact that he hadn't taken action against the woman before she had the chance to hurt the people he loved.

"Has Evelyn said anything?" Holly asked.

Ty shook his head. "Not since she came back from the hospital. They drew blood on her, and according to the doctor, it sounded like Evelyn was higher than a kite. High doses of opioids in her system as well as barbiturates and marijuana."

She shook her head, but she didn't look surprised. "I'm sure she and Robert were using together. It definitely helps to make sense of some of their erratic behaviors."

He looked over at her and noticed the way her blond hair was loose around her shoulders in a long cascading wave. Her makeup was on point and, aside from the cast on her arm, she seemed perfectly put together. For the first time since he'd come back into her life, she seemed to be at peace. Unfortunately, he had a feeling he was going to cause an upheaval and he didn't like himself for it. Yet, they needed to find answers and sometimes a little upheaval wasn't a bad thing.

"She'll be going through detox soon, and before she does, we need to get her to start talking." He caught Holly's gaze and sent her a wordless question.

"Seriously?" she asked, having been able to read it on his face. "You want me to go in there? Don't you think that it will send her over the edge? She's a drug addict and unpredictable."

He reached down and took her hand in his. "This isn't like before. You are in a controlled environment, she is handcuffed and I'm right here. All I want you to do is get her talking. I know it's unconventional, but I want to see her response to you."

She stared at their entwined hands like they were a lifeline, and she was on a sinking ship. He hated that look on her face. The last thing they were was sinking. No, they were rising on the tide of change and finally breaking through the storms that had ravaged her life. She was strong and together they would grow even stronger.

"If you don't want to do it, you don't have to—no pressure. If you choose to go in, I'll be right by your side."

That made her entire demeanor change. She lifted her

chin and her shoulders straightened. "Okay. I just don't want to be in there alone with her. I know what she is capable of," she said, lifting her casted arm.

"If I have my way, you'll never have to do anything in your life alone again." He winked.

Her mouth dropped open and she tilted her head slightly, reminding him of a confused puppy. She was no puppy, but he loved that expression. He'd do anything to see that expression every day. There was nothing better than surprising her.

"But you haven't...you don't love me." She smiled widely as if she knew, without him saying, what he was thinking and feeling.

In this moment, he wasn't about to break that seal. He sent her what he knew was his most charming smile. "We will see about that. Besides, you're still on trial," he teased.

The door to the interrogation room opened, and Stowe walked out and into the large chamber that looked into both interrogation areas. He was shaking his head and looking dejected as he closed the door behind him. The reality of the moment pulled them from their playfulness, and Ty was reminded all too much about everything that was at stake.

If they did not get a confession from Evelyn, or something from Valerie that tied her or her sister directly to Moose's death it would be extremely hard to prove. They could get Evelyn on charges of breaking and entering and assault, maybe even more if she had been the one who had shot at them; but until they got all of the reports back from the crime lab about the knife and their findings, it would all depend on this interrogation and their ability to make her and her sister talk.

The good news was that with those charges alone, he could keep Evelyn in jail for at least as long as it would take to get the results. As such if Holly didn't want to go in there, or if she got in there and needed out right away, there was still time. However, he also knew that Rebecca, Moose's mother, was waiting on answers.

It was his hope that after today, he could go to her and tell her that the person responsible for her son's death was behind bars and would go to trial for their crime.

"Valerie's refusing to talk besides saying that she had nothing to do with the murders. The only good news is that she hasn't lawyered up," Detective Stowe said. He stepped beside them in front of the two-way mirror and looked in on the interrogation room with Evelyn.

She was staring down at her hands, where the shackles where pinched tight around her wrists. She moved her arms slightly, like she was trying to make them less uncomfortable, but they had been designed to hurt. If she hadn't been combative with Holly and him, he wouldn't have required that she keep them on, but as it was, he didn't trust her. Especially given the fact that she was on drugs.

"Is it okay if I go in and talk to her?" Holly asked. "Maybe I can get her to start talking. At least, I want to ask her why she did what she did." She looked over at Ty for reassurance, and he sent her a comforting smile.

He was proud of her for her strength and tenacity.

"She did what she did because she is a criminal, but I get what you're saying," Stowe said.

His ego must have been slightly bruised that the big-city detective couldn't get the small-town drug addict to open up and he was aware their only shot lay with Holly. Ty shouldn't have found a glimmer of joy in it, but he couldn't help himself.

"She and I will go in together," Ty said, getting in front of the man's possible arguments against them talking to Evelyn.

"If you think you can get her to talk, knock yourselves out. But do remember that the county attorney and the judges will be watching all of the footage from inside that room. Everything that happens will be heavily scrutinized." Stowe shot them a deathly serious look.

Ty appreciated what the guy was saying, but he needed no reminder. "I'm hoping that given the fact that she may have played a role in a law enforcement officer's death, that this is one trial that will go a little smoother."

"As I'm sure you know, before we make any assumptions, we need to make sure that this is the person or persons we are looking for in relation to your friend's murder." Stowe paused. "I know we've talked about it a little bit, but I still can't understand why she would have targeted Moose."

"He was having a relationship with Valerie—that's why we brought her in to talk. She may give us some hard evidence connecting either her or her sister directly to these murders. When we brought her in, she admitted she'd been sleeping with Moose. Who knows? Maybe that's why Evelyn thought she needed to act. Maybe something in her drug-addled brain told her that her sister needed to be saved." Ty shrugged.

"Again, you're making assumptions. We need concrete evidence or the woman in there—" he motioned toward the interrogation room where Evelyn sat "—to start talking. If we don't, she may very well get away with murder."

"Let me at her," Holly said, stepping toward the door. Stowe looked torn but gave her a stiff nod as he touched the doorknob. He pushed the door open and waited for Holly to follow Ty into the room.

Evelyn looked up from her dedicated study of her handcuffs. Her expression darkened, and her lips pulled into a twisted sneer. "Couldn't get enough of me?" she challenged.

"If I remember correctly, I put up a pretty good fight," Holly said.

"But I see you're wearing a cast," Evelyn countered, with a malicious grin.

Holly moved to the chair across from the woman and sat down. Ty stepped behind her, covering her back and giving her his support.

"How's your head doing?" he asked, motioning to the back of her head where he had smashed the computer into her. "Got a little bit of a headache?" He really couldn't help himself this morning.

"Gloat all you want," Evelyn said, a twisted smile on her lips. "I still got what I wanted." She looked directly at Holly. "Though, if I'd gotten everything I wanted, you'd be dead, too. Actually, both of you would be. If only I had killed you the first chance I had."

Holly looked at her. "What do you mean?"

"When I had Robert's truck. I should have waited and been more patient, but I had to shoot. I couldn't stand watching you two smiling together. You're the worst kind of woman. You deserve to die."

She tried to hide her surprise and hatred toward the woman who not only despised her, but also wanted her dead.

"What did I ever do to you?" Holly asked. She leaned against the table like it could support her emotionally as well as physically.

Ty dropped his hand to her shoulder, giving it a gentle squeeze and hopefully letting her know that she was doing well.

"If it weren't for you, Robert would have loved me."

Holly made a choking sound. "You do know that I was not interested in Robert in any way," Holly said, putting her hands down on the table in a symbolic gesture that she was telling the truth. "He wouldn't leave me alone and I didn't want anything to do with him romantically."

Evelyn started to rock back and forth, but Ty wasn't sure if it was because of a nervous tick or the fact that she was likely coming down off drugs.

"You're a liar." Evelyn's movements grew more erratic. "Robert told me what a liar you were. He told me all about what you did to him, and how you wouldn't leave him alone. He even showed me all the times you called and texted him. You loved him. You know you loved him." The woman's words came out faster and faster almost in tandem with her rocking.

"I talked to him because I worked with him." She paused as she pulled up memories. "He didn't take it well when I ignored him, and he would get more and more incensed the longer I went without responding." Holly sounded as though she was struggling to control the emotions she was feeling from leaching into her voice.

Ty hated that she was struggling. "Evelyn, why were you on the mountain the day of Moose's death?" He was aware that he was leading her, but this wasn't a courtroom and he simply needed her to acknowledge the fact that she had been in proximity at the time of the murder.

"Robert had told me that she was up there. He was really upset. She hadn't responded to him the night before she went missing. She's so selfish. She ruins everything." Evelyn was staring back down at her cuffs.

It didn't escape him that she was talking about Holly like she wasn't in the room.

"But why were you on the mountain? Were you looking for Holly?"

She looked up at him, anger filling her face with hard lines. "If I killed her, I could solve everything. I could do what needed to be done. Robert would be free of her, and he'd never be held accountable for her death. What I really wanted was for no one to find her body."

"So, you went up on the mountain with the intention of killing Holly?"

"Yes." Evelyn spat the word in anger. "And I would have. If that reckless man hadn't gotten in my way. I didn't plan on using that knife on him. I wanted to make it look like Holly had gone to the woods and slit her wrists. Everything went wrong, though."

"Did you cut his throat?"

She blanched. "I stabbed him first… He tried to fight back, but I got the knife out and moved at him." She paused, looking toward the mirror. She smiled, wickedly. "It is strange how easy it is to cut someone's throat. The windpipe feels like cutting through a rubber band."

He hated this woman. She was the epitome of a criminal. She was so self-righteous and so filled with anger and hate, there was no rehabilitating her. When she went to prison for this, which she would, he'd make sure of it, she needed to never get out.

"He told me what you guys were there to do, and I knew I was too late. But I knew I'd get another chance, I just had to be patient. I just had to watch." Evelyn's rocking slowed. "That's why I went to her house… If only you hadn't been there…" She sounded aggrieved.

Her breaking into Holly's garage and his now made a little more sense. It was warm and sheltered from the elements. From within, she'd probably been able to watch anything she wanted through the kitchen window.

In fact, he wasn't sure that she couldn't have seen into his breakfast nook from nearly the same vantage point. He didn't want to ask if she had watched them that night when he'd been with Holly. He wouldn't let this mad woman steal anything from that wonderful night. She'd already taken enough from their lives.

Holly said nothing.

"Was the knife we found in the garage the same knife you used to kill Moose?" he asked, his stomach roiling at the thought but he forced himself to remain stoic.

"I thought it was a nice touch."

"Why did you leave it?" he pressed.

"I wanted Holly to know I was coming for her—and that I wasn't afraid to kill again." She looked over at Holly and sent her a vicious smile.

Holly turned away.

As much as he wanted to protect Holly, he appreciated that she was here—her presence was helping. Evelyn hated her so much that she only cared about hurting her, and in doing so she was digging herself a deeper prison sentence.

"And why did you kill Robert, if you loved him so much?" he pressed, though he didn't have a clue whether or not Evelyn had played any role in the man's death.

Evelyn threw her hands up as high as she could with them being bolted to the table. "I didn't do that. I could never have hurt him. I tried to make him stop. But all he could do was talk about her. He said she was never going to take him back. That I'd screwed everything up." Her words came out fast. "I tried to get the gun out of his hand." Evelyn's voice cracked with emotion.

The way she spoke made him think that she was likely telling them the truth.

"Before I could get the gun out of his hand, he'd had it against his chin and..." Evelyn stopped talking. "I tried to help him. I tried." Tears welled in her eyes, and a single droplet spilled down her cheek, making her appear almost human.

Ty reached for the box of Kleenex and pushed it over in the woman's direction. He knew he should have expressed sorrow for the woman's loss. He'd been present at more than one callout that had ended in a self-inflicted gunshot wound. It was grizzly. It was something that a person could not unsee. However, these two individuals, Robert and Evelyn, had been playing an evil game.

Though they had all experienced so much tragedy and loss, Ty was relieved. They finally had some answers and a path for recourse. There would be justice for his best friend's death and the attempted taking of Holly's life.

Chapter Twenty-One

The one aspect of the case that Holly just couldn't come to terms with was the flowers that had been sent to her office. The card had been handwritten and it was a woman's scrawl, but that had likely been written by the florist and not the sender.

Evelyn wouldn't have sent those flowers. Robert may have, but she didn't know. She wanted to find out. Maybe they could go to the florist and ask questions. Then again, she wasn't sure she would want to know if Robert had sent them. If he had, it would ruin cut flowers for her, forever.

As she stood in the hallway outside of the interrogation room, her body started to shake. Ty wrapped his arms around her from behind.

"You're going to be alright," he cooed, as though he understood. "You've been through a lot today and your body is just adjusting to the stress of the environment. Sometimes I get the shakes, too. You'll be okay, though. I've got you."

He brought her so much comfort.

She turned to face him, without breaking from his embrace. "Someone sent flowers to my office with a note that read 'I'm sorry.' They showed up the day after Moose's murder. I have no idea who they were from, but I need to know."

Ty nodded.

"I know I shouldn't be worried about such a trivial thing, but it's the one point I just can't make sense of. It could have been Robert, but he was never one to apologize to me for anything. If anything bad happened, it was always my fault. And he had to have sent them before the time of his death. Which means he may not even have known about Moose's death or what Evelyn had done."

Ty gently rubbed his thumb over her back. "What you're experiencing is totally normal. It's part of that stress response, kind of like your shaking. You're myopically focused on a detail. But don't worry, we'll get it solved. It will be easy enough to figure it out. All we'll have to do is talk to the florist and track down financial records."

She appreciated that he didn't make her feel wrong for what she was feeling and how her body was reacting. He was such a kind man. And she appreciated that he wasn't pressuring her to feel a certain way or respond a certain way. He just accepted her for who she was and what her body was capable of handling.

"Why don't I go in and talk with Valerie. I need to get to the bottom of everything that she's played a role in here, if she sent her sister out on that mountain she should be up on charges." He pulled her into his arms and took a deep breath like he was smelling her hair. The simple action helped her stop shaking. She caught her breath as he just stood there and held her.

It was so easy to love him. And now that this was all bottled up maybe they could have a real relationship.

She would leave that ball in his court. This was his job that was at stake, and she certainly understood the upheaval that was occurring within his department right now thanks to the evidence tech's role in these two deaths in the community. The only good news was that it didn't appear that Valerie had actually pulled any triggers, figurative or otherwise. That had all been Evelyn.

Calming, she looked up into his eyes. "Go get this done so we can really start our lives together." Maybe she wasn't gonna leave it in his court after all. She had changed, but she'd never silently stand by when she wanted something, especially something as important as him.

As she spoke, he threw his head back with a laugh.

"Our lives together?" He gave her a cheeky grin. "You haven't even told me you love me yet."

Her face flamed with embarrassment.

"Just get your butt in there." She giggled. "Before anyone can say anything, we need these answers."

He rounded his shoulders and looked like a dejected schoolboy. He sent her a wide grin over his shoulder as he made his way into the interrogation room where Valerie sat waiting. The door closed behind him, and as quickly as the door closed his smile disappeared. She was amazed by how quickly he could go from laughing to all business. It had to come with the job.

He sat on the sofa of the soft interrogation room. The room was far more decorated than the one her sister was currently occupying; Valerie was sitting on a leather sofa that had a coffee table in front of it complete with a stack of magazines and two boxes of Kleenex.

She watched from the other side of the mirror as Valerie reached forward and grabbed a tissue and dabbed at her nose. A fresh stream of tears poured down her face. "I'm so sorry," Valerie said, sobbing.

"So, your sister was very forthcoming with information. Do you wish to tell us your side of the story?" Ty asked.

Valerie sobbed harder.

"I know how hard this is, Valerie. But I also know that you understand how important it is to tell us the truth. Especially now, after you've been less than forthright throughout this investigation." He sighed.

As she watched him work, Holly realized how much this had to bother him. She'd been so concerned about her own feelings and the effect talking to Evelyn had had on her, but she hadn't even considered how he would feel going into that room with his coworker. Yet, if anybody was going to interview her it did make sense that it was him. No doubt the other detective would get his chance, but Valerie had always seemed to like Ty.

Unfortunately, it seemed that she had loved her sister more.

"Evelyn was using my computer, and I had no idea. She was all over that call with Holly when she went missing. She asked me a ton of questions." Valerie hiccupped and dabbed at her nose. "I didn't know Robert's relationship with Holly. Well, not until I got home that night. Evelyn had gone off the rails. She was screaming and yelling, and she was covered in blood. I forced her to tell me what had happened, and when she told me about Moose…" Her body was rattled by sobs.

"I was so angry with her." She gulped for air. "I told her I never wanted to see her again."

"Did you have any role in Moose's death?"

"No!" she said, looking up at him through tear-filled eyes. "Absolutely not. I *loved* him. I think that was part of the reason Evelyn killed him. We were talking about getting married."

Ty put his hand on Valerie's shoulder like he wanted to comfort her in some small way. "If you knew Evelyn had been snooping on your computer, and you knew that she had played a role in your future fiancé's death, then why did you not turn her in?"

She fell forward, cupping her face in her hands in shame. Her shoulders were curled, and sobs rattled through her. "I should have. I wanted to. I just…" She sobbed. "I'm so sorry."

"Is that why you sent the flowers to Holly?"

She nodded. "I planned on turning Evelyn in. I felt horrible for your loss and what my sister had done. That's when I made the order, but I couldn't turn on my sister like that and by the time I changed my mind, they had already been delivered." She ran the back of her hand under her nose, giving up on her tissues. "I mean, I know I should have turned her in, but the damage was already done. I didn't want to lose my sister, too. She and Moose were the only people I really had in my life…in my corner."

He shook his head. "It doesn't sound like your sister was ever in your corner. In fact, it could be pointed out that your sister seems to be your worst enemy. Not only has she cost you your job, your pension, your integrity—and the man you love—but she may have cost this entire department millions. Every case you've ever worked on will now come under scrutiny."

Valerie gasped. "Oh, my God."

She covered her face and succumbed to her tears.

Holly had liked the woman, she really had. She was pleasant and sweet when they'd met earlier this week. To think this woman had basically undone all the good work of the department—even if she had done it all in the name of the love for her sister.

Epilogue

It had been nearly twelve ugly and beautiful months.

Because Valerie had worked on the investigation of Moose's death, she had been convicted of obstruction of justice and accessory to murder, after the fact. Last week, she had been sentenced to three years in the Montana Women's Prison in Billings.

Valerie had gotten a reduced sentence because of her candor and willingness to work with county attorney's office in clearing her past works and limiting the effects of her criminal behavior.

Evelyn was found guilty in district court for one count of deliberate homicide. It carried a minimum sentence of life. She would never leave prison.

At least the sisters were in prison together—there, they could continue protecting one another.

Holly was just getting up for the morning when Ty walked into her kitchen. Since they'd been dating, he'd been staying over more and more often. She loved every minute of him being there with her.

He moved behind her as she cracked an egg and poured it into a bowl to scramble. Ty wrapped his arms around her and nuzzled his face into her loose hair. "Good morning, babe. I was going to make you breakfast today."

"You don't need to cook for me, babe," she said, turning and giving him a quick peck to the cheek before cracking another egg.

"I have plans for your birthday. You can have breakfast, but I am going to need you to go along with my plans for the rest of the day." He rubbed his morning stubble against the edge of her ear.

"Only if you say what I want to hear," she teased.

"I will tell you all day, every day. I love you, Holly Dean."

Her heart leaped into her throat. She would never get tired of hearing him say those words. "I love you, too."

She put down the eggshell and washed her fingers off in the sink and dried her hands. Turning around, she smiled at him. He reached behind his body and pulled out a box from his back pocket.

The little box had a red bow and there were skis on the wrapping paper.

"Ah, it's so cute," she cooed.

"You haven't even opened it yet," he said with a laugh.

"What is it?" she asked, going to the table to sit and open it up.

"It's your first present of the day."

She moved from foot to foot in excitement. "What? You didn't need to get me anything. I don't need anything more—I have you, that is the greatest gift I could get." She smiled at him as she sat down.

"You are so full of it this morning," he teased, coming over and kissing the top of her head.

"I mean it," she said, trying to sound affronted by his teasing.

"Birthday girl, I'm the lucky one." He put his hand on her shoulder. "Now, open up your present."

She pulled off the bow and slowly opened the package, taking her time.

She lifted the top of the black cardboard box. Inside was a set of ski tickets to the local resort. "Ah, babe, thank you. When are we going?" she asked.

"Today, but you're not done opening presents. Wait here," he said, putting a finger up and motioning for her to stay.

He stepped to the window and waved toward the garage. A few seconds later, Rebecca came in. She had a huge, mischievous smile and a cake in her hands. "Hi, kiddos!" she said, sounding so excited. "Happy Birthday!"

"Thank you!" Holly said, excited to see the woman who had become a major part of their life and regularly popped in with "extra" food she'd made for dinner. She loved the woman almost as much as she had loved her mom.

Ty took the cake and set it on the counter. "Thank you for doing this, Mrs. Dolack. We're glad to have you here for this." He sent the woman a wink.

"You know you can call me 'Mom.'" Mrs. Dolack waved him off. "And I'm just honored you called. I'm happy to be a part of this. Our little family," she said, her smile growing impossibly wider. "Oh, Holly, here is the best part." Mrs. Dolack reached out the door behind her. Then she lifted a new set of red Rossignol skis and handed them to Ty.

Holly set her ski passes down on the table and cupped her hand over her mouth. "Oh, guys, I love them!"

"You're welcome. I know how much you've been wanting to get back out there." Ty handed her the skis.

He really was the best man she'd ever met.

She sucked in a breath as she looked at the freshly waxed

skis. "They are beautiful. We'll have to go this week. Maybe after we can go to Mom's for some hot cocoa."

The older woman nodded, but she put her hand over her mouth like she was struggling to keep a secret.

"Wait." He smiled. "First, look at the binding."

She lifted the ski to look. There at the end of her right ski's binding was a small velvet box. She stopped and stared.

"If you don't like it or whatever, I can take it back," Ty said.

She could barely move as she stared at the velvet box. Was he doing what she thought he was? If so, this was going to be the best birthday of her life.

He dropped to his knee in front of her. "Holly Dean, you are the love of my life. When we were kids, I knew I wanted to marry you, but I thought it was crazy. If only I had listened to my heart, then we could have saved so much precious time…"

She put the back of her free hand over her mouth, staring at him in front of her. Her eyes welled with tears. She had never known she could be so happy as she had been since he had come back into her life, until now.

"Holly," he continued, "we grew up together and it is my hope that we can grow old together. Will you marry me?"

She nodded. "Yes. Absolutely, yes. You are my best friend. I wanted to marry you when we were kids, too."

He opened the box. Inside was the most beautiful Black Hills gold ring that she had ever seen. It had leaves of green and pink roses in the gold. At its center was an inset diamond. It was stunning.

Ty slipped it on her finger. It fit her just as perfectly as the man who was giving it to her.

"I am yours," she said, staring at him.

"As I am yours," he said, standing. "Ski buddies, forever."

Their kiss was deeper than the meeting of lips. In that moment, the people who had lost so much over the years and had been left stranded alone by life came together as a family.

* * * * *

If you missed the previous books in
Danica Winters's series, Big Sky Search and Rescue,
look for these titles, available now:

Helicopter Rescue
Swiftwater Enemies
Mountain Abduction